Insurgent

(Bones, Book Two)

Characters by Name

Danny "Bones" O'Brien:
Irish Catholic.
Lives by respect.
Known to shake a man's hand while having him
shot in the back of the head.
Moretti's right-hand man.

Paul O'Brien:
Irish Catholic.
Oldest brother of Danny and Samuel O'Brien.
Smart.
Straightforward family man.
Mayor of Postings, New Jersey.

Samuel O'Brien:
Irish Catholic.
Youngest brother to Danny and
Paul.
Kind soul.
Works in construction.
The "angel" of the brothers.

Johnny "Sweep" Dolffi:
Catholic.
Childhood best friend to the brothers.

Cleanup man—gets rid of the bodies.
Big guy.
Eerily quiet.

Carson "Trig" Kelski:
Lived in the same foster home as Sweep.
Trigger-happy.
Will shoot you for looking at him wrong.
Psychopathic tendencies that he tries to contain by
popping a rubber band.

Bexley Walker:
Moved in next door to the brothers at age eleven.
Mom died of cancer, resulting in her moving across
town to live with her uncle Hale.
Started dating Danny at age sixteen.
At eighteen, their relationship ended horribly.
Works at a flower shop in Postings.

Ma:
Grandmother to the O'Brien boys.
Sweet woman.

Moretti:
The boss.
Put a hit out on the people who murdered Danny's
parents.
Took Danny under his wing at a very young age.

Editor: Paige Maroney Smith
Cover designer: Cover It Designs
Proofreader: Julie T.
Betas: Crystal Jones
Monica Lewis

Chapter One

Bones
2015

I sit at the bar, watching the game on TV as people drink and carry on behind me.

"So, he asks, 'What do you think your girl fantasizes about while she's fucking you?'" Yaps says to Sweep.

Yaps is a big mouth. Talks too much so we call him Yaps, short for Yapper. He hangs out here at my bar and shoots the shit with the boys. Also loses a lot in poker and does too much cocaine, but he makes me money, so I tolerate him. But right now, I'm watching this shit show of him eating olives and talking with his mouth full.

It's slightly annoying me.

Trig looks around the bar, bringing his beer to his mouth. "And what did you say?"

"I shrugged and said, 'I don't know. What the fuck do you think she fantasizes about?' You know what that motherfucker said?" He grabs an olive from the bowl he requested from Mae, popping it into his mouth and chewing.

Sweep picks his favorite nut from the dish on the bar, clearly uninterested like he is with a lot of things. If it doesn't involve sports and beer, Sweep doesn't give a shit.

"I give up," Trig says.

"He said, 'Me,'" Yaps says, chewing with his mouth open.

I take a sip of my beer.

"So, I hit the fucker upside the head with a beer bottle." He laughs, showing us what's in his big fat mouth.

"You know what?" I say to him, grabbing my cigarillo case from my jacket's pocket.

He looks at me, his chest still bouncing because he thinks he's so funny.

"What, Bones?" he asks, helping himself to another olive.

I light my smoke. "I've sat here and watched you for five minutes talk and talk and eat olive after olive and talk and talk." I make circles in the air with my hand, then point to the bowl. "You stick the olive in your fat mouth, and you keep talking like there's nothing in there. Didn't your ma teach you any manners?"

His eyes look from me to Sweep.

"Don't look at Sweep. I'm asking you a question. Did your ma teach you any fucking manners?"

"Yes, B…"

I hold up my hand. "You've still got food inside your mouth. You spit when you talk. How about chew the shit and then speak? Also, you do too much. Hitting the man with a beer bottle 'cause he was telling you a joke."

He swallows. "You wouldn't have done the same if someone was talking about your girl?" he asks.

"I don't have a girl."

"That's right. You're the no-commitment type. Guess I would be, too, if I did the shit you did. Enemies would come after her like white on rice." He chuckles, taking a big swig of whiskey, signaling for Mae to get him another.

My jaw tightens, and my blood turns icy at the lack of respect this motherfucker has. What does he know of the things I've done?

"Trying to teach me about manners. I got fucking manners. What manners do you got, huh? Mae, can a man get a drink around here?"

"Yaps," Sweep warns.

Yaps looks over at him. "What? The man's saying my ma didn't teach me any manners. I ain't got a right to be upset about it?"

I hit my smoke as Mae walks over. She looks at me. I nod, telling her it's fine. Give the man another drink. Silence hangs in the air, and then as if he realizes what he's done, he turns to me.

"Fuck, I'm sorry, Bones. I've had too much to drink." He holds up his hands, putting his glass of liquor down.

I nod and pick up my beer. "A toast," I insist. "May you be in heaven a full half hour before the devil knows you're dead."

Sweep eyes me, and we three clink glasses. I cast my eyes back to the TV, calming the madness from the shit I have to deal with sometimes. Yaps should really consider that prayer.

A lot has changed over the last nine years. I own a bar now, and people like this dumb fuck occupy it. It's a cover-up for all the money I make. I gotta have some kind of job, or the government starts getting suspicious.

When Mickey died, Moretti named me his right-hand man. He also gave me the name Bones, Johnny the name Sweep, and Carson is known as Trig because he'll shoot your ass without a second thought. He's trigger-happy.

At the time, I didn't want the title. I started seeing things differently when Mickey got popped by those meth heads. All of a sudden, this life I'd chosen didn't make much sense.

One minute, we were on a run. We were headed back and talking about doing business in Atlanta, and the next he was bleeding out in Johnny's backseat. The way his eyes looked when he was about to die.

I saw regret.

I saw pointlessness.

Insurgent

And now he's buried in the Pine Barrens. Nothing but dirt, overrun by the worms.

Shit like that will fuck with you. You can't look a dying man in the eye and not come away with something. It sticks with you, like a new layer of skin. It changes you.

I went from a boy to a man that day.

I was considering getting out. I was thinking about changing my path, but I messed up.

I'm not big on regret, but when it comes to her... yeah, there's some guilt.

Chapter Two

Danny
2006

Prom.

"Fuck, man." I run a hand from my nose to my mouth, exhaling before I grab my phone from my pocket. It's dead. It's almost ten at night, I was supposed to pick her up at five this afternoon.

"What?" Johnny says.

"I forgot about prom."

"Oh shit," Carson says. "Man, she's going to be pissed."

"No, she's going to be done," I say. I don't have a charger in Johnny's car. "Let me get one of your phones." Carson hands me his. I flip the thing open and dial her number. It goes straight to voicemail. "You gotta take me to her house."

"Looking like that?" Johnny says. "You still got Mickey's blood on you."

"I don't care. I've got to get over there."

"All right," he says.

I hit the dash. "How the fuck did I forget about this?" I hit call again.

"Um, I don't know, maybe because we were almost killed, and a man was dying in the backseat of this car?" Carson says. "Who the fuck is thinking about some stupid-ass prom?"

"I warned you about this," Johnny says.

I look over at him. "Love, it's me. I'm sorry. I'm so fucking sorry. I'm on my way. We got held up. I'm sorry," I say again before I snap the phone shut.

"I told you she didn't fit into this lifestyle," Johnny says.

"Do we fit into this lifestyle?" I ask him.

He narrows his eyes at me.

"We just saw a man die. And for what? Some homemade liquor and smack?"

"You're letting Bex cloud your vision, Danny."

"No, I think for once in my life, my vision is perfectly clear. I'm not sure about any of this anymore."

"Moretti just made you his right-hand man," Carson says.

"Yeah." I nod. "Know what that means? A fucking death sentence."

Neither of them says anything, and I'm sure it's because partially they know I'm speaking the truth. What are we doing this for? What's the point anymore?

Chapter Three

Bexley
One month two days missing

The sound of a truck pulling up has both Danny and
me lifting our heads. I hear the door shut, but like
always, the truck stays running, and moments later,
I hear keys.

The stranger steps inside, holding two coats.

"Thought you two might like a little extra
warmth."

Danny scoffs. "Tell me," he says weakly. "How
is your plan working out?"

I instantly grow worried. Why is he provoking
this man?

"Just fine," he says.

"Are you lying?" Danny asks, clearly not
believing him.

"Come on, Bones. Do you really want to fuck
with me?"

Danny tilts his head up, looking at the man's
mask and the coats in his hand. "I must have really
done something, huh?" he says lowly.

The stranger tenses.

"I must have ruined your whole life for you to go
to all this trouble." Danny shakes his head. "Tell

me, man who's so big and bad he has to hide behind a mask and voice disguiser. What was it? Did I fuck your wife? Did I kill your brother, your father? What did I do for you to keep us here like your little pets?"

The man drops the coats onto the floor, going to the window.

Both Danny and I watch him.

"I've always thought you were a smart man, Bones. But it appears that you're not."

He gazes out, and Danny looks at me. I try to tell him to stop this madness. He could kill us both.

But Danny, being the stubborn asshole he is, just smirks. I look away from him, staring at the floor and wishing the man would just leave.

Faintly, I hear the sound of something snapping. I look back at Danny, who's grown white as snow.

The man turns around. "You need to remember who's in charge, Bones. You need to understand that you're no longer calling the shots. You're a dead man." The stranger walks over to us. Grabbing my hair, he pulls me out of the way. I kick my feet, clutching his hand and wincing as little pieces of hair get ripped from my scalp.

"You motherfucker!" Danny says, spit flying from his mouth. The stranger shoves me toward the wall. I rub my head as he walks over to Danny, leaning down in his face.

"You keep your mouth closed." He reaches behind him and pulls out a knife. Danny's knife. The one he apparently took. Grabbing Danny's jaw, he squeezes. "Or I'll cut your fucking tongue out," the stranger says. He reaches behind Danny and cuts the ties off his wrists before doing the same with his upper arms. Danny's arms fall as if they're broken. He cries out in pain.

"Get the fuck up," the man orders after he reaches down and cuts the zip tie from Danny's ankles. But Danny doesn't get up. He tilts and falls flat on the floor. His face hits the wood hard enough to knock him out.

"Jesus Christ. This is the man you love?" he asks me. "This sorry fucker?" He kicks Danny and I scream, thinking about his already bruised ribs. I crawl over to him.

"Stop!" I say. "Just stop."

He laughs. "You're just as stupid as I was. Do you know who this man is?" he asks me. "Do you have any idea the ruthless things he's done? The people he's killed. How can you stand by a man like this?"

"Did you not stand by him?" I ask. "Surely if you know him as well as you act, then you've been witness to his crimes or, in fact, have done horrible things yourself. Look what you're doing to us."

He exhales, walking over to the window. Looking out, he says, "I did stand by him. I would have died alongside him, but he's the reason for everything that's gone to shit in my life."

"How?" I ask. "How is he the reason?"

He turns to look at me. "Even after all these years, you still love him."

My throat dries even more than it already is. Why does he keep saying things like that? What does he care if I love Danny or not? My mind starts to play tricks on me. Could this be...? No, no. Not Samuel. Why am I thinking that? Good God, he would never do this.

It's not possible. I saw what happened. I was there. There's no way. I'm going crazy. I'm losing it. "I care for Danny. But you're wrong about the love part. I don't love him. The man I love is no longer here."

He laughs. "And that's because of him." He nods at Danny passed out on the floor. Walking over to me, he reaches behind and cuts my ties, too. I gasp as my arms come forward. My shoulders ache painfully. I can feel it getting worse every time he cuts them so we can use the bathroom.

"Get him up." He walks out and I look down at Danny. I move the hair from his face, running a finger over his beard.

"Danny. Wake up."

His eyes flutter open, and he turns over onto his back. His bones pop as he groans in agony. Stretching his leg out, he quickly sucks air in.

"Cramp," he says through his teeth. "I'm going to kill him." He holds on to his ribs.

"You're too weak, Danny. We both are."

His eyes go to me, blood and dirt cover the skin I can see, and we share a look that says we might not make it out of here, but I don't swim in it.

"Come on," I urge before my hand goes to my mouth. "Oh God." I look at his wrist when his sleeve rides up. "Your wrist, Danny. It's swollen and looks infected." I touch his forehead. "You're burning up."

"I'm fine," he says. "Help me up."

"You're not fine. God, we really are going to die out here."

"Don't talk like that," he says.

I wrap my arm around his waist and help him stand as he grabs ahold of the chair and straightens up. The stranger walks back into the house with some firewood. He tosses it into the wood-burning stove in the middle of the room. After lighting some paper and fat lighter, he puts them in there, too. "I'll leave some wood here," he says. "Bexley, you'll stay untied. You can keep the fire going. It'll be no fun for me if the two of you freeze to death."

"Why do you care about the cold now? It's been freezing the whole time we've been here."

"Want me to take it all away?" he asks.

I shut my mouth.

"That's what I thought. Be grateful, bitch. Come on, Bones. Let's go take a piss."

Chapter Four

Bexley
2006

I stare at the clock on my phone, constantly opening and closing the thing. It's almost five.

I haven't heard a word from Danny since this morning. I've showered, shaved, and had my hair and makeup done. I even got my nails and toes painted. It's been a day of prepping. I exhale, walking over to the window and looking out as the sun warms my face. This is important to me. He'll show.

I lean against the window, and I wait.

I wait, I wait, and I wait.

Uncle Hale knocks on my bedroom door. "It's getting late. You think something might have happened to keep him from coming?"

"I called. His phone is going to voicemail."

Hale nods. "I'd hate for you to miss your last chance at prom, Bexley."

I swallow the tears I so desperately want to let loose. Taking in a deep breath, I straighten my back. I will not let Danny ruin this for me. But I can't go alone. I try to think of anyone who might not have a date, but I come up empty.

Insurgent

God, I'm so mad right now I could scream! How can he do this to me? How can he stand me up like this? How can he say he loves me, and not show up? Red-hot anger rushes through my veins, giving me courage I didn't know I had.

I will go alone.

I will hang out with my friends, because this is my last year. This is it for high school and memories. Afraid I'll burst into tears if I'm alone in my car, I ask Hale to give me a ride.

Before we leave, Trinity pulls me to the side.

"So, look, I'm not the best at giving advice or anything, but if I could go back and talk to my younger self, I'd tell her one thing. Enjoy every moment of this, because one day it'll be nothing but a faded memory. I can see you love Danny, and so can your uncle, but you're eighteen. You have a full life ahead of you. Grab it and run, girl."

I smile at the woman I've grown fond of. She can't cook worth a shit, she's a little quirky with her fifty something bracelets and wild curly hair, but she makes my uncle happy and really, that's all we want in life, right? For the people we love to be happy. To be loved, fully. Not only does she put a smile on my uncle's face, but she's known from the start that he and I are a two-package deal, and she's not once made me feel like I was an issue.

"Okay," I say. "I'm doing this for older me."

She winks. "There you go."

Hale doesn't say anything about Danny as we ride, and I'm grateful. I couldn't handle a serious conversation right now. Instead, he tells me about his prom and high school days, and he talks about Mom and how much fun they had growing up. It takes my mind off of Danny, if only for a little bit.

When we pull up at school, music flows from the open doors. Balloons are swaying in the wind, and everyone I've gone to school with for the past four years has a smile on their face.

I look back at Hale.

"Life is about choices, Bexley. I think you're making the right one here. Go in there and have a blast. Drink the spiked punch, dance with your friends, and remember this night with a smile."

I give him one, even though on the inside I feel sick and completely heartbroken. Taking a breath, I open the car door and step out.

"Call me if you need a ride," he says.

"Thank you," I reply. I exhale and make my way in. The music is loud, and the place is crowded. I look around the room at the dancing lights and the full tables.

"Bexley," I hear. I turn to look and see a group of my friends.

"Where's your date?" Jessica, a fire-red redhead who sits beside me in algebra, asks.

"Family emergency," I lie and inner me rolls her eyes, because she's sick of lying for this guy.

"That sucks."

"Life sucks sometimes," I say.

She lifts a brow. "Well, seems like you need a drink." She pulls out a flask and hands it to me.

"Careful. Chaperones are everywhere."

I nod, quickly taking a sip of the whiskey and instantly regretting it. I cough and hand it back to her, wincing.

She laughs. "It's rough, huh?"

"A little," I agree.

My eyes scan the room for more familiar faces, and then I spot Danny's brother, Samuel, with a group of his baseball buddies. Wow. He cleans up nice. I didn't get to see his brother in a suit, but this is probably the second-best thing. I slightly shake my head.

No more Danny. Get him out of your mind.

At that moment Samuel spots me. His face lights up and it makes me smile.

"Hey," he mouths.

"Hey," I mouth back. He looks at his buddies and then back at me. With a slight tilt of his head, he signals for me to meet him by the drink table. It's sneaky, and it almost makes me smile.

"I'll be right back," I tell Jessica.

"Okay," she says.

Walking toward Samuel feels like slow motion. There's this force, trying desperately to drag me back. I can feel the pull on my skin, the shake in my bones, but I clench my jaw and move forward.

"Life is about making choices, Bexley."

Am I making a choice?

I believe I am.

Being with Danny is like watching a tornado. It's fascinating. It's a rush, a wonder even. So, you stand there staring, until something flies by nearly hitting you, and then the danger really sinks in. This could take you down.

Danny is fun and exciting and, God help me, I love him, but after the storm passes, there's nothing but rubble and destruction. And I'm afraid I'm going to be the house left with only a foundation.

Truth is, I feel like I've been holding my breath, waiting for Danny to mess up.

It shouldn't be this hard, should it? Relationships should be easier. Danny's made me feel unimportant.

Never let anyone make you feel second-best.

When I make it over to the table, Samuel gives me his Samuel smirk and I exhale the air that's been held captive inside my uneasy lungs. There's a flutter of pain between them still, though, and I know that's not going away any time soon.

I plaster on a smile for this boy, even though it feels like I've been stabbed.

He frowns. His eyes scan the room before landing back on me in an oh-so knowing way.

"Where is he?" he asks, his voice a bit deeper than I recall the last time we spoke. Wait, when was the last time we spoke?

I shrug, heartache winning this game I didn't want to play. A tear spills from my eye, and Samuel watches it slide down my cheek.

Shit, shit, shit. Stay strong, Bexley. You can do this.

I swallow the enormous lump of agony in my throat as my hands begin to shake uncontrollably and a line of sweat rolls down my back, puddling at the bottom. My knees feel like piled ash, one wisp of the wind away from their demise. My spine prickles, my stomach swarms, and saliva forms thick in my mouth. I look up to see the bathroom, covering my mouth with my hand as I run toward it.

I hear my name coming from his lips as I find a stall and rid my body of toxic anguish. I heave until my ribs ache and sweat forms on my brow. I hear chatter from other girls in here, but they have no idea how real life is. They're in this plastic bubble of Lip Smackers lip gloss and Victoria's Secret Dream Angel Halo. They're clueless.

"Hey, you can't be in here," one of the girls says.

"Sorry, one of my friends is sick. I just want to check on her. Can you ladies give us a moment, please?" I hear Samuel, and I smirk regardless of my situation. He's a sweetheart and a smooth talker.

Their chatter leaves the room, and I've never been more grateful for Samuel than I am right now.

"Bexley." He taps on the door.

I exhale. "Yeah."

"You all right?" he asks.

I scoff. "Define all right? I'm staring at the toilet in a prom dress. My boyfriend is out doing God knows what. He may even be dead." My soul slams to the bottom of my heart at the thought of that and I choke on a sob.

"Can you open the door?" he asks.

I don't answer. Instead, I stand up, reaching to flush the toilet before sliding the latch.

Samuel stands with his hands slid into his pockets. I'm ready for the I-told-you-so speech. I brace myself for it, but it doesn't fall from his lips.

He gives me a sad smile. "I'm sorry," he says.

And I never expected that.

"You're sorry? For what?"

"That my brother is hurting you."

"It's not your fault. Danny is...Danny." I shrug.

He shakes his head. "I've heard that all my life, you know? Danny is Danny." He scoffs. "It's fucking bullshit."

I blink, surprised to hear that language coming from Samuel.

"Danny doesn't have to be the way he is. Everyone always accepts the heartache he gives, forgetting that he doesn't have to give it. He could care a little more about the people who love him and not be such a screw-up."

I don't say anything, because he isn't wrong.

"Look, I've got a date out there. She's probably wondering where I ran off to. I just want to make sure you're all right."

"I'm okay," I say. "I think I'm gonna get out of here."

"Did you drive?" he asks me.

"No. Hale dropped me off."

He nods. "Well, I can give you a ride home."

"And leave your date? No, I'd never ask you to do that."

"It's not a problem. We're not going out or anything. She's just a friend."

"Does she know that?" I ask.

He grins. "I hope."

I exhale.

"I'll go talk to her. Can you meet me outside?"

"Okay," I say gently. Samuel leaves the room and I walk to the sink, looking at the mascara under my eyes. I run a hand under them, rinse my mouth, and head outside.

It takes a little bit for Samuel to walk out, so I sit on the bench, watching as people filter in and out. Some are clearly a little tipsy. Others are teasing the teachers we've all grown to know so well, and here I am sitting alone in a polka dot prom dress with the taste of vomit in my mouth.

I look at my phone and see it's dead. I wonder what time it is. I was late for prom, and I only stayed long enough to have a sip of whiskey, cry, puke, and cause someone to lose their date.

What a shit show my life has become.

"Life is about choices."

My heart slows its beat, my chest aches. All I want to do is curl up in bed and sleep, but I'm afraid that won't be easy.

I've never felt this type of pain before. It's untouchable. Sure, Danny has made me sad, he's worried me, but knowing it's the end? Knowing I can't go on like this? It hurts worse than anything I've ever experienced. I feel defeated.

"You won, Danny O'Brien. You've finally pushed me away," I whisper.

"You ready?" I hear behind me. I look up, seeing Samuel with a loose bowtie around his neck.

"I'm sorry I ruined prom for you, too."

He scoffs. "These things are lame anyway. You wanna go grab some food or something?"

I shake my head. "Truthfully, I just want to get out of this dress and forget this whole day."

He nods, and a second later he reaches his hand out to help me up. I take it, and he makes a show that I'm heavy, pulling me up a little too hard, so I end up bumping into his chest, which makes me laugh. His hand goes to my waist, and his expression changes from playful to serious.

Insurgent

My eyes look to his before bouncing down to his lips. For a moment, I feel my age. Eighteen, in a pretty dress at school, with an average boy who likes to play baseball. My mind replays the last few years, going over every special moment I've had with Danny. From the birthdays to the car rides we'd take listening to music and smoking.

The fights and the makeups. It rewinds all the way back to Thanksgiving when this boy right here invited me over. I'd made a choice that day to take a chance on Danny. I wouldn't trade our time together for anything, but I know now I made the wrong choice. I understand that there was never going to be a future for us, because a normal life doesn't play into Danny's way of living.

Paul's words from the last heartache Danny caused me roll through my thoughts.

"Danny will always be married to the streets. You'll always be wondering where he is or if he's coming home."

I've been a silly girl, swept up in a dangerous romance. Playtime is over. Danny is a criminal and I'm afraid, that's all he'll ever be.

I clear my throat and move my face away from Samuel's. "You know he'd kill us both."

Samuel shakes his head. "I'm not a little boy anymore, Bexley. I can take my brother."

I look him over for a moment. Samuel is fit, having played sports nearly his entire life. Danny does his own working out, push-ups and pull-ups in the backyard at his lake house. It would be a close fight. Both guys could hold their own, but Samuel couldn't take Danny's gun, and truthfully, I don't think Samuel could take Danny, period. Danny's ruthless; he'd fight to kill.

"I would hate you two to fight over me. Let's just go."

"Are you going to end things with him?" he asks as I start to walk toward the parking lot.

"I don't know what I'm going to do." I look down when he grabs my arm, spinning me around to face him.

"Don't be stupid, Bexley. You know this will never stop. He will always hurt you."

My façade breaks and my voice cracks. I cover my mouth as tears fill my eyes. "You don't think I know that? You don't think I'm dying here?"

Samuel looks guilty, and he pulls me close to him. "Shh, Bex. Don't cry."

But I can't help it. I sob uncontrollably into his chest, gripping the material of his suit. In the school's parking lot, pain-filled teardrops cover my face, and I hold on to Samuel because he's the only thing keeping me from falling.

Chapter Five

Bones
One month two days missing

I'm torn in two. Ripped from the inside out. My boy? I don't understand. Where did I go wrong with him? How did I take everything from him? Bexley keeps trying to get me to talk, but I can't right now.

I was a little harsh when I told her to be quiet earlier. But she doesn't get what's going through my mind right now. I've been betrayed. I've been gutted. I never in a million years would have seen this coming.

I would have bet my life on it. I try to recall everything we've done together. All of our conversations. I keep coming up empty-handed. I don't know what I did. I would have died for this man.

And now I'll have to kill him.

There's no other way.

I have to get us out of here. Bexley's right. I'm burning up and my wrists are battered. I need to stop moving them. Maybe if I stop irritating them, the swelling will go down. Bexley convinced Trig to give me some ibuprofen and that might have

been his biggest mistake. He tossed her half a
bottle. I'll make sure to take a few every four hours.

This has to help.

It's all we have.

Chapter Six

Danny
2006

I don't have a plan for what I'm going to say to Bex when we pull up. I just know I want to beg her to forgive me. I fucked up. I should have called. I should have… What should I have done? I was on a run. I was with my guys and shit went wrong. How could I have known this was going to happen? I had my tux. I told her this morning I would be there to get her, because that was my intention.

I'm out of my mind with worry at this point. My thoughts are scattered, my chest burning with the fear she's going to tell me to leave her alone and never come back.

I look down at my clothes. Fuck, I'm a mess. Johnny's right. What the hell are they going to say about the way I look? I have blood on me.
I think for a moment.

"Pull over," I say.

"What?" Johnny looks over at me.

"Just stop the fucking car." I hop out. "Pop the trunk." I hurry to the back and grab the spare tire and walk up to the backseat window. "Carson," I say, hitting the glass. "Change out that right tire."

I leave the spare leaning against the car, walking back to the trunk.

"What the hell for?" he says, getting out.

"Just do it!" I say. "Hurry up." He rolls his eyes and I grab the crowbar as he gets the jack.

Johnny gets out. "Have you lost your goddamn mind?"

"Move back, Carson." I rare back and hit the windshield on the passenger side.

"Man, what the hell?" Carson says.

I hit the front headlight, too, and then I grab my knife from my side and hold out my palm. With an inhale I slit my hand open and hold it over the hood and windshield, letting blood drip.

I put my knife back.

"Oh," Johnny says. "We hit a deer."

"Big motherfucker," I say with a slight smirk.

Carson bends down, working on the tire. "You two are fucking crazier than me. All this for a chick."

After the tire is put on, we continue to Bexley's uncle's house. I wrap my hand with a towel as we near her house. I hold my breath, and then I see a car in the driveway, and I see her and...Samuel?

"What the hell?" I say.

"Danny, man," Johnny says.

I pull on the handle when Johnny stops the car and I jump out.

"The fuck is this, huh?" I ask, walking up to them sitting on the trunk. Samuel straightens and gets off the car. This is way over the line.

"You taking my girl to prom?"

"Danny, don't," Bexley says, sounding exhausted and climbing down, too. But I ignore her, shoving him.

"Answer me, motherfucker."

He stumbles back. "I took her home because her boyfriend bailed on her."

I don't think. I don't hesitate. I punch my brother square in the jaw.

"Danny!" Bexley screams.

I hit him again before he has time to fight back, connecting with his nose and sending him to the ground.

"The fuck you thinking, Bexley? I asked you to stay away from him. I told you what would happen."

She shakes her head, eyeing me in horror. "Look at you," she says. I stare at her, and as my eyes see the mascara trailing down her cheeks, and the dress she picked out, that she looks so pretty in, I swallow sick regret.

I look down at my hands, still covered in blood and mud from Mickey. I see my brother on the ground holding his nose.

"Love, I'm sorry."

"Don't you call me that." She clenches her jaw.
"Don't you ever call me that again. I waited all day
for you. I put on this silly dress and got my hair and
makeup done, just so you could make me cry it all
off."

I walk over to her, but she shoves me away,
causing me to put my hands up in surrender. "No!"
she says as more tears fall. "I told you... I told you
not to make a fool out of me." She shakes her head,
her hair falling behind her back. "I'm done. It's
over between us."

"You don't mean that," I say. "I got held up.
Something happened."

"Something always happens," she fires back,
looking at my clothes. "Good God, Danny. What
the hell? What is that? Blood?"

"We hit a deer." I point back to the car.

"You hit a deer?" she asks.

"Yes. That's why we got held up."

She shakes her head, rolling her eyes at the same
time before focusing her attention on my brother.
"Samuel, I'm sorry I dragged you into this. Go
ahead and get out of here. I'll call you later," she
says before turning toward the house.

But I follow. "You won't fucking call him later,"
I tell her.

"I'll call whoever the hell I want Leave,
Danny."

But I still follow as she hits the step and opens the front door. "Bexley," I say, desperation in my voice. "Please. I'm so sorry. I…I'll leave it all. I'll get out of this. I promise. I'm done. After tonight, I'm done. I realize now I don't want to be without you. This is all fucked up."

She turns around. "You realize *now*? After everything we've been through. It took this for you to see you don't want to be without me?"

I search her face, feeling my own tears, and my heart feels as though someone's crushing it with a hydraulically powered plate. I search the ground for answers, but there's nothing, only dirt and grass. I'm losing her.

I've lost her.

The one good thing I had.

I don't give a shit that Johnny and Carson are watching. That I just broke my brother's nose and he's witnessing this whole shit show. I drop to my knees, lower my head, and grovel. "Please, baby. I'll do anything."

"Don't do this," she says.

I look up at her. "Let's leave. You get enrolled into a good college somewhere and do your photography, and I'll find a job. I'll be a better man."

Her tears fall like rain, and my own heartbreak drips from my jaw.

"Danny," she says in agony, covering her mouth.

"She told you to go," I hear behind her. "She's given you too many chances. You're no good for her."

I lift my chin and stand up. "This is none of your business."

Her uncle shakes his head. "Look at you, son. Look at your clothes and your face. I don't want my niece involved in anything you've got going on. You need to leave before I call the cops."

"You can't keep me from her," I say.

"Oh yes, I can," he says.

I straighten my back and ball my fists.

"What are you doing?" he asks. "Bexley, get behind me."

I look at her and watch in utter horror as she moves behind her uncle. Rage replaces heartbreak, and I reach out and shove her uncle. He holds on to my arms, but I fight. He pushes me backward and I swing on him, my fist connecting with his face.

"Danny!" I hear behind me, recognizing Johnny's voice.

"The cops are on the way," a woman says from behind Bexley.

"That's assault, my boy. You're going to jail," Hale says, touching his jaw.

I blink, wiping my face with the back of my hand, realizing what I've done by the look on Bexley's face. I messed up. I messed everything up. "Bexley," I say, reaching for her.

"Stop!" she says. "Just stop. Why are you doing this?"

"Because I love you!" You're all I've got. You're all that matters."

"Then why?" she asks, moving around her uncle, who tries to stop her, but she shrugs him off. "Why didn't you show up? Why don't you show up?"

I grab her hand, gripping it with both of mine. My eyes scan hers and I try to tell her, to connect like we do. "Marry me," I say quietly. "Let me show you I can be better."

I hear sirens and a car pull up. Doors open and Johnny says my name again, but I don't look away from Bexley.

Her beautiful face shatters. "No," she says as tears roll over her lips.

I kiss her hand in agony, just before words are spoken to me from behind. My arms are snatched back, and I'm taken away. I look ahead, lifting my chin as the cops toss me into the car.

And as I stare at the seat, I make a promise to myself.

I will get her back.

Chapter Seven

Bexley
One month two days missing

"I know who it is," he finally says. It's been hours since the stranger left, and Danny hasn't spoken a word to me.

"You know who who is?" I ask with narrowed eyes.

"The guy holding us here."

My eyes scan over his face. "Who?"

"It's Trig."

"Trig?" I ask, confused. "I don't know anyone named Trig."

"Carson," he says. "It's Carson."

"Carson?" I look to the floor. "You're talking about Carson? The one who always hangs around you and Johnny?" I remember Danny asking Johnny where Trig was after the funeral. I was too upset to care who that person was then.

"Yes, Bexley. Keep up here."

"Hey, don't get pissy with me. How do you know this?"

"The rubber band, didn't you hear it?"

I shrug. "I…I guess…I didn't really pay attention. I was too worried about him cutting your tongue out."

He shakes his head. "None of this makes sense. He's my boy. He's been with me since we were teenagers. We took out…" he stops talking, looking up at me.

We don't say anything, because what's there to say? Danny almost admitted murder in front of me. The cold truth sinks its nasty teeth back into my spine. I'm here because of this man.

This man, who is a murderer, who has done things I couldn't imagine nearly all his life—I fell in love with him, and I tried to look past it all, but no matter how far you try to run from it, the truth catches up to you.

"Why do you all have these nicknames?" I ask.

"It's just something we earned over time."

"What do they mean? Bones, Sweep, and Trig?"

"Different things," he says.

"Enlighten me."

He exhales. "I've broken a few people's faces over the years. Sweep…well, he does a lot of cleaning, and Trig is fast with a gun…too fast."

I shake my head, still not clear on it. So, they call you Bones because you break people's bones? Like you broke Samuel's prom day."

He winces.

"And Johnny cleans a lot?" I narrow my eyes, moving them back and forth over his face. "You mean he cleans up the things you do."

"You asked," he says.

"I'll do better in the future," I reply, deadpan.

He clears his throat, looking down. "I've always regretted that day," he says moments later.

"What day?"

"Prom. I never meant to hurt you, Bex. Of all the things I've done...that's at the top."

I scoff. "You've killed people, and standing me up is the thing you regret most?"

"Losing you," he says and the way he says it...if heartbreak had a voice, it would sound like his. My throat dries, and my heart pounds a little harder. I get a feeling in my chest that only can be described as coming home. Some people say home is a place, but I think home is more than sheetrock and insulation.

Home is a feeling. Comfort, ease. Danny has always done that for me. He looks at me, as I look at him tied to the chair. We've both aged, but Danny's looks are loyal. He's always been a heartthrob.

"I meant it, you know?"

And I do know. I've thought about that day several times throughout the years. How he begged me not to end it. How he got on his knees despite everyone around us. How he asked me to marry him with the idea of us running away and living some fantasy life. Me taking pictures and him…I wouldn't have any idea what he would have done. I wanted that more than he could ever know. But I realized the truth.

"You couldn't have done it," I say.

"I could have."

I smile, but it's not from happiness. It's because he knows just as well as I do that he would have been miserable.

"I could have tried," he says.

"And you would have eventually hated me for it. We just weren't meant to be, Danny. And that's all there is."

Chapter Eight

Bexley
2006

Completely heartbroken, I watch as they take Danny away in the cop car. Should I have stopped this? Should I have forgiven him and none of this would have happened? I wipe my face, gazing at the blue lights until they disappear from my sight. *Why couldn't he have shown up?*

That's all he had to do. All I wanted was to go to this stupid prom with my boyfriend. But even as that thought runs through my mind, I know it's ridiculous. Danny isn't your average boyfriend. He's a criminal. He's always going to be a criminal.

He hit his brother and my uncle. He's no good for me.

And it hurts.

God, it hurts.

"Bexley," Uncle Hale says. "Come on. Let's go inside."

I look out at Samuel, who's also staring at his brother with his hands slid into his slacks' pockets. "I'll be inside in a minute," I say, walking away from the steps. I stop and slip my shoes off, leaving them on the sidewalk as I make my way out to Samuel.

He turns when he hears me coming. "Hey," he says.

I give him a nod, my throat closing up as I think about everything that just happened. I put my hands on my face, looking down the road and trying to gather my thoughts. I give myself a pep talk.

You are stronger than this. Yes, you love him, but sometimes love isn't enough, girl. You knew from the beginning what he did was going to end you two and yet, you still decided to take a chance. You'll never have to say what if, but you can say I tried.

Move on.

My heart crosses her arms and hangs her head. How do you move on from someone like Danny? He's been my reason since I was a little girl. And now I'm just supposed to let it all go?

I can't seem to get my mind and heart to agree on anything right now. "I'm sorry," I say to Samuel.

He looks down at me. "You have nothing to be sorry for."

I scoff. "Please, just stop being so nice. You wouldn't even be here if it wasn't for me."

"No, I wouldn't be here if Danny would have shown up."

I blink, looking at his nose. "Is it broken?"

"Think so," he says. "It hurts pretty bad."

I make a face. "I can't believe he hit you."

And then I follow it by saying, "Yes, I can."

"Yeah, I expected it. I just thought I would have fought back. Something made me stop, though."

"What?" I ask.

He exhales, touching his nose gently and wincing. It's swelling, but not bleeding anymore. "He's my brother. As much as I hate the things he does, you're his and I've broken a secret code by taking you home."

"A secret code?" I say. "This is ridiculous. You only gave me a ride, Samuel."

He chuckles. "But my intentions aren't good, and I think you know that."

I blanch. I've always known Samuel's liked me, and Danny even told me one time that he was in love with me. I guess I see it. I've just been…ignoring it? I love Danny. I always have, and I've been so blinded by the love I have for him that I didn't want to see anything else. I hate to think that way, but it's the truth. I've been a foolish girl.

"Yeah," I say. "I guess I do."

He doesn't speak for a minute, and then he says, "I better go."

I nod. "Okay. Well, thanks for everything."

"Anytime, Bex. I'll see ya."

"Bye, Samuel."

Chapter Nine

Bexley
One month two days missing

I've been staring at the walls, thinking back on our past. Thinking back on when we were two kids in love. I shouldn't be thinking about any of this, but it's all there is to do. Danny slept a little, and when he woke up, I gave him some more ibuprofen. Taking the water bottle from his lips, I ask, "So, what are we going to do about our situation?"

"We've got to get out of here," Danny says.

I laugh. "I don't think that's working out too well."

"I don't need your smart mouth right now, Bexley."

This pisses me off. "Oh. I'm sorry. I guess I should be nicer to you, being you're *not* the reason we're in this situation." I walk over to the window, looking out into the thick forest. A bird lands on a branch, fluttering his wings, tilting his head in a jerky way before taking off. God, how I wish I were him right now. I'd fly away from all of this. I'd start a new life.

"How long were you in jail?" I ask quietly.

"What?"

"Prom night. When you hit my uncle and broke Samuel's nose," I toss that back in there, and I know it's because I'm intentionally trying to hurt him.

Being petty isn't a cool thing to be, but sometimes it's all we've got.

"Only hours," he says. "Moretti got me out."

I look back at him. "A few hours?"

He exhales, looking up at the ceiling. "There's so much you don't understand about my world, love."

"Don't call me that," I say acidly.

This time he laughs, focusing his attention on me. "You don't get it, do you? It doesn't matter who you married. It doesn't matter how many years have gone by with us being apart, you still belong with me."

"Oh dear God in heaven, if you believe that, you're more insane than I thought."

He chuckles, looking toward the floor. I twist the top of the water bottle, exhaling as I turn toward the window again. And somewhere…deep inside, I know he's right.

"How did you do it?" he asks.

"Do what?" I murmur, looking out at the trees as they sway.

"Move on so quickly."

I take a moment before I answer him, letting the question hang in the air, like dust particles floating through the rays of the sun. Thinking back on all the

years that have flown by, I recall the utter
heartbreak I felt when he was taken away in that
police car. The regret I felt even after all he did. I
wanted to go after him, to tell him that it would be
okay.

But I forced myself to be strong. I forced myself
to go on even when all I wanted to do was curl up
and die. How do you survive letting go of the only
thing that made sense to you? How do you ever
truly move on when part of your soul is snatched
away? I'm not sure I ever did.

I was alive, but I wasn't living. Not really. I
loved my husband and I tried to make a life with
him, but it was never... it was never what Danny
and I had, and I know he knew that, and that's also
something I have to live with. I should have let my
husband go. I should have let him be with someone
who could love him as much as he deserved.

I look back at Danny. "What makes you think I
moved on quickly?"

His eyes bounce to the cold hardwood below my
feet. "I watched you for a while. You seemed fine.
You seemed..." I watch his eyes move as if he's
trying to think of the right word, and then he says,
"Peaceful."

I shake my head. "Looks can be deceiving,
Danny." I move away from the window, sliding
down to the floor, hating how bad my shoulders still
ache regardless that I'm no longer tied up. My mind

goes back to a question I asked him after the tragic incident at the flower shop. I asked him if he was watching me. He didn't respond, which told me he had been. Has he always watched me? I shake that from my thoughts, getting back to the conversation at hand. "I called you about a thousand times."

"I had no missed calls from you."

"That's because I always hung up."

He lifts a brow, the dried blood on the side of his face cracking. "I wouldn't have answered anyway," he says.

"Why? You begged me not to let you go and you wouldn't have answered my phone call? You watched me from afar and you wouldn't have wanted to talk to me if I called you? You're contradicting yourself. You just told me you could have changed, that you could have lived a normal life with me, and now you're saying what? That you know you couldn't have."

He exhales. "I'm saying I would have tried. But you told me no, and so I did the only thing I knew to do. I became the person I was always meant to be."

"How?" I ask. "How did you become this person?"

He tilts his head slightly, lifting his shoulder. "I was always strong-minded, Bexley. I was determined in everything I did. In loving you, in climbing the ladder to success."

"Okay, well, we know you failed at the first one. So, how did you win at success? Better yet, what is success to you?"

"Success is different for everyone. For me, it was not being the losing guy. It was waking up every day and making money and doing whatever I had to do to protect the way I make money."

"And that meant hurting people."

He tilts his head. "If they got in my way, then yes."

I don't say anything to that. While Danny was apparently diving deeper into the crime world, I was just trying to survive without him.

Chapter Ten

Bexley
2006

I stand in front of the flower shop window, watching as the rain falls outside. It rivers down the glass in small streams before it drips onto the windowpane. It's been a slow day, heavy storms on and off. I hold my phone in my hand, my eyes bouncing down to the screen, looking at his name.

It's been two weeks. I haven't heard a word from him. We went from seeing one another every day to this. I press call, and then before it even rings, I hang up. This has become an unhealthy habit and so has listening to the voicemail he left me that night.

Over and over, I listen to his voice. As if he's died and I'll only ever hear it from my phone's speakers. It's as depressing as it sounds. It hurts as much as if he did die. I can hardly eat or sleep. I'm just here. Letting one day pass before another.

The first few days were the worst. I cried myself sick every night. Thankfully, that has stopped, and now I just stare at the ceiling wondering who I should hate more. Him or myself?

Both had a hand in destroying me.

I wonder how he is. Does he hurt like I do? I've almost driven to the lake house so many times. I've made it halfway there before I pulled over and banged my fist on the steering wheel, crying until I couldn't breathe.

Surely heartache is the worst pain there is. There's no cure; nothing you can take to ease it. You just have to zombie through. I hear footsteps behind me, and I look back at Billie, the owner of A-Street Flower Shop. She's wearing jeans and a loose fitted cream sweater. Billie's well into her thirties and has been great to me during my teenage heartbreak. She tells me one day I'll wake up and it just won't hurt so much anymore. I long for that.

"Bexley, I'd like to talk to you," she says, dropping a crate onto the cement table in the center of the shop.

I fully turn around as she starts removing flowers to cut the stems. "Okay?" I ask, nervous. Maybe my moping has been too much. I hope she isn't firing me.

"I've been talking with my husband and I've finally got him convinced. We're buying a farm."

"Oh," I say, surprised. This is not the conversation I expected. "Congratulations?" I say questionably, because who wants to do all that work?

She laughs. "Thanks. I know it's going to be a lot of work, but I've always wanted one. It's been my dream, actually." I walk over to help her, grabbing some vases from the bottom of the table and walking behind the counter to fill them with water.

"So, what does this mean exactly?"

"This means, I won't be here hardly at all and I need someone to run the place. I know you're about to be finished with school and you're probably thinking about colleges." She looks back at me.

"Which, by all means, shoot for the moon, girl, but I wanted to toss an idea by you. Since I won't be here, I wanted to see if you would run the shop for me. Full-time. I would increase your pay substantially.

"You would be in charge. Of course, you could hire someone to help out when you need time off and that wouldn't cut into anything you earn."

I place the cut flowers into the vase, trimming down any excess leaves that fall below the waterline.

"Think on it. I know it's a lot."

"Why would you trust me to run this place? I mean, don't get me wrong, I'm flattered, but I don't have a degree or anything that qualifies me to run a business."

"You have something that, to me, is better than a degree. You have experience and a drive to learn. You've been a big help to me, and I trust you."

"Thanks," I say.

"You're welcome. Take some time to think about it. Rome wasn't built in a day and neither will this farm, so we've got a little while before things change dramatically, and when you decide...if the answer is yes, I'll teach you everything you don't already know. I would pay you well, Bexley. You would be helping my dreams come true, and I hope to eventually expand this place and bring in the fresh produce I grow and the eggs my chickens will hatch. It would be great," she says excitedly.

"I'll definitely think on it," I tell her.

"Good." She nods. "Now let's get these finished up and put in the fridge. That bride I'm dealing with is a complete nightmare," she says. "If they look even a little wilted, I'm afraid she might burn the whole place down."

I laugh, and for the first time in a while, it feels real and I feel like I have a little hope that things just might be okay.

As I'm about to leave work for the day, my phone rings. I nearly drop the thing and break it to pieces to hurry and see who it is. When I see it's my uncle, I feel my whole body droop. Did I really think it was going to be Danny?

"Just checking in," he says after I answer. "The storm's going to hit us hard in a little while."

"I'm leaving now," I say

"Good. We'll see you in a bit. Be safe."

I hang up and slide my phone into my pocket, thinking I should throw the thing away so I can get over this shit already.

"Hey, Bex," Billie says as I'm about to walk out the door.

"Hmm?"

"It's going to be all right. We all eventually get over our first love, and we go on to realize that maybe we are better because it happened and because it's over. Every ending is a beginning."

"Yeah," I say, trying to muster up a smile.

"You need to get out. Enjoy life. Be a teenager."

"I'll try that," I say, giving her a wink before I push the door, thinking how I wish people would stop telling me that. Be a teenager, like it's something you must take advantage of before it's yanked from you. Before you have to grow up and live in the real world.

Well, I'm already living in the real world. I open my umbrella and walk to my car. I open the door and get inside, tossing the wet umbrella into the passenger side floor after I close it. The rain picks up, hitting the roof of my car. I start it, place my hands on the wheel, and drop my smile.

I'm alone now. Nothing but the rain and me. I'm grateful for Billie's offer. It's like a dream really. I love this side of town, so that's a plus. I'll talk it over with Uncle Hale and see what he thinks. I exhale, put my car in drive, and pull out onto the road.

I grip the wheel when I hear a loud pop from the back of the car and then it starts wobbling. Dear heaven above, not a flat tire in this rain. I pull over and put my emergency lights on. Placing my forehead on the steering wheel, I groan in defeat.

I should have been paying better attention when Hale tried to show me how to change a tire. A knock sounds on my window, and I jump, looking out. Samuel stands with a raincoat on, but still getting soaked.

I roll my window down. "What are you doing?" I ask him.

"It looks like you're in an unfortunate situation." He lifts a brow. "Need some help?"

"Uh, yeah, seems I do."

"Got a jack and spare?" he asks.

"Yes. In the trunk." I grab my umbrella after I pop the trunk and get out.

"You can stay in the car."

"I'm not staying in the car while you get all wet changing my tire."

"I'm already wet, Bex," he replies. I ignore him and I watch as he grabs the jack and tire out. My eyes look to his work boots.

"What are you doing on this side of town?" I ask.

"Work. We're building a new house close to here. I had to come and get some supplies."

"Oh," I say, hunching my shoulders, trying to stay as dry as possible and trying to cover him. I remember now. Samuel started working a construction job a while back. "You guys build houses in a storm?"

He rotates the lug wrench, removing the bolts from the blown-out tire. "Well, the outer shell is up," he says. "We're working on the inside."

"Right," I reply, like *of course*.

I don't say anything else so he can work without me bothering him. Samuel is good with his hands. He's a man's man. Sweet enough, and so cute. He's always been a looker, but so have his brothers. My heart wilts as I think about Danny, but then I also think about Paul, who I haven't spoken to in a long while. "How's Paul?" I ask.

"He's good. He's got a girl now, seems to really like her."

"Really?" I ask with a smile, genuinely happy for the boy I've always thought of as a brother.

"Yeah. He's doing what he's always wanted. I guess he and Danny are." He turns back to look at me at the mention of Danny, and I bite my inner cheek, trying not to show how much just the sound of his name affects me. His eyes look to my lips before he focuses back on his task.

He tightens the last bolt and drops the jack, standing up. "You doing all right?"

I shrug. "Could be worse."

He nods.

I swallow, not sure I want to ask this question, but I do it anyway. "How is he?"

His eyes narrow slightly, like he isn't happy that I inquired. "He's fine. Doesn't come by much anymore. Moved all his things out of Ma's. We figured he had his own place already anyway."

I look down at the spare tire. I wonder if he's removed all the photos he hung. If he's gotten rid of my things at the lake house, where we spent so much time together. I guess I should have gone by and picked some stuff up, but really none of it was mine. He bought it all, even the film in my cameras.

God, his face that Christmas when he surprised me with the lights and the presents under the tree. He did it all for me.

Thinking about those things… it makes me want to say screw it all. I can live with the bad side if I can get pieces of that Danny. I just want some of him. I know I sound pathetic, but I can't help it.

"You need to move on, Bex. He has."

My eyes bounce to him. I could slap him. *He has.*

"If it were that simple, Samuel, I wouldn't have even asked about him. I hope no one ever does to you what he's done to me, because then you'll feel what I do. This pain is indescribable."

He smirks. "Yeah, I'm just standing out in the rain changing your tire for the hell of it."

"What?"

He shakes his head. "Nothing. You're good here." He places the old tire and tools in the trunk and shuts it.

"Take care," he says. I watch as he walks away from me, the rain still falling heavy around us. My mind tells me once again that I'm a fool. My heart's chasing after the wrong boy. But who on this god-forsaken planet can control that stupid muscle? I climb back into my car and head home.

Chapter Eleven

Bones
One month three days missing

My girl's done well making sure to give me the ibuprofen every four hours. The swelling in my wrists has gone down, making it easier for my plan to work. I didn't want to tell Bexley when she asked what we were going to do about our situation because I didn't want to give her false hope.

I wiggle my hands, wincing when I feel my flesh break once again, but I need the blood for lubricant. With a hard tug and some groan-worthy pain, I slip my wrist free from one zip tie before doing the same with the other. I exhale before breathing in and then I yank my arms outward, breaking the ties that bind my upper arms to the chair.

The moonlight shines in the room, so it has to be the middle of the night. Well after midnight, I'd presume. I can't see my watch, so there's no way to tell. My wrists throb and I feel the blood dripping down the front of my palms.

The fire in the stove still burns, keeping us warm, but the stranger didn't leave much wood, so it'll be out sooner or later. Luckily, we only had severe snow fall right when we got here. Other than that, it's been cold, but not below freezing. I look down at Bex sleeping on the floor. I remember hearing rats here the first few nights, but they've disappeared, thankfully.

I watch the rise and fall of her back, the sound that slips past her lips when she breathes out. I remember how she used to sleep beside me at the lake house. Always on her stomach with one leg bent. I loved feeling the warmth of her next to me and the way she'd jump a few times before finally dozing off. I'd smell her hair and study her face.

I think about how different my life might be if I would have gotten out all those years ago when I went to Moretti. Maybe she'd be sleeping beside me at the lake house now. Maybe we'd have some kids.

I wonder why she and… I stop myself from thinking that. Their marriage ate me up enough to think about them sharing a child. Her walking around with another man's baby. Even if it would have been a part of *him*, I can't handle it. My chest aches for the great man we lost. We had our issues, but I loved him.

I sniff, rolling my neck and moving my arms to allow circulation, and I think about that day when I almost got myself killed because I foolishly thought it was going to be that simple. I was just a kid, only twenty-one and I'd already felt like I lived a lifetime. Now I feel as though I've lived several.

Chapter Twelve

Danny
2006

"I want out," I say, walking into Moretti's office.

He looks up at me, fresh out of jail, dirt caked on my clothes and blood still on my hands.

Moretti reaches up and grabs a cigar from his box. He twirls it between his thumb and finger.

"Sit down," he says calmly.

"I don't want to fucking sit down. I'm done. I came here to tell you that." I was confident in what I was saying, thinking just because I said it, it would be.

His eyes focus on mine. "I said *sit* down." His tone was harsher, his face darker, and that's when I realized this wasn't going to be as easy as I thought. What I wanted meant shit.

I narrow my eyes slightly, feeling the stretch in my skin. I look down at the chair I've sat in more times than I can count over the last eight years I've been working for this man. Reaching out, I grab the thing before reluctantly taking a seat.

He studies me for a moment. My heart pounds, and for the first time I feel how powerful this man really is. "Do you remember the first day you walked in here?" he asks.

I nod.

"And do you remember what you asked of me?"

I feel my brow furrow. "I think I've repaid you for that."

"You do?" he asks, acting surprised. "Okay." He says those words with a smug look on his face. "Nugget!" he calls out. Nugget walks in moments later. He looks from me to Moretti.

"Pull out your gun," Moretti says.

My mouth dries.

Nugget does as he's told.

"Point it at Danny."

I look straight ahead, feeling the cold stare down from the gun pointed at my head, knowing Nugget would like nothing more than to pull the trigger.

"You'll never repay me," Moretti says to me. "I own you, just as I own every other man out there in that room. That's what happens when you ask me for a favor. I thought you knew that. I thought I saw that in you the first time you walked into my office. You hardly had hair on your balls and yet you came in here acting as though you were a grown-ass man."

I don't answer. I've done a lot of dirty things for him. I've killed to protect his business. To protect him from the people out there who'd like nothing more than to see him dead. He got my friend a home so he wouldn't have to leave Postings. He got me out of jail. So what? Now I owe him my life?

Fuck.

"I had the people killed who took your father and mother from you," he says. "Do you know what I did to those people?"

"I don't remember asking you to do it."

"Careful, Danny. You have a gun pointed at you."

I lift my chin, feeling as though my teeth might break from the force of my jaw.

"I've had men killed for less than what you're doing now. Do you understand? You made a choice when you were thirteen. You and Johnny decided you wanted to be in this lifestyle. You don't get out. This is it. This is your life. The only way you'll be done with it is when that little black heart of yours stops beating.

"Now I can make that happen or we can continue with business. Which would you like?"

I'd like to cut your eyes out and shove them down your throat.

Of course, I don't say this.

"You're having second thoughts because of Mickey?" he asks.

"He died for nothing," I reply.

"No. Mickey knew the risk. He's always known."

"You didn't even blink an eye," I say.

Insurgent

"What the fuck's gotten into you? Huh? You get your dick wet a few times by that girl and now you've grown all soft on me? Where the fuck is Bones, the boy known around Postings for breaking the bones in people's faces?"

I've heard people call me that around here, but it's the first time Moretti has acknowledged it.

"Where's the hard ass that works for me? The dark prince? The one I made my right fucking hand?" He slams his fist down on the table, yanking his cigar from his mouth. "Get the fuck out of here," he says to Nugget.

Nugget drops his gun, and I turn to face him. He eyes me, and I lift my lip a tad. Moretti wasn't going to kill me. He's just trying to prove a point.

I think.

The door shuts and Moretti grabs a box of matches from his desk and strikes one, lighting the cigar. Woodsy tobacco fills the room as I look down at the matchbox. My mind is overrun with thoughts and the reality of my situation really sinks in.

This is my life.

There's no way out but…death.

Bexley doesn't want me anymore, so what else do I have? I've only known violence and crime since I was a boy.

She's done the right thing. She'll go on and have a happy life. Until I get things in order, and then I'll come for her.

But for now, I'll continue the only way I know how. From this day forward, I'm no longer Danny O'Brien, boy sick in love with a girl who doesn't fit into the dark world I live in.

I'm Bones.

And that's just the way it has to be.

"Look, you won't see that girl again. She clouds your vision."

My eyes jump to him. Moretti's hair is slicked straight back, and he's wearing a dark suit with a gold watch. He's always looked the part he plays.

"That's an order. Be done with her. If you need something to fuck, grab one of these girls around here." He hits his smoke. "I need you to say you hear me on this."

"Yeah, I hear you."

"Good." He nods. "Things are changing. We've got to think smarter." He sits back in his chair, twirling a gold diamond ring on his finger. "I realize we gotta use these damn cell phones, so we'll use nicknames because the feds are listening. I notice them more and more on the streets."

"Okay, I'm Bones, so what will I call you?" I ask.

"Boss," he replies. If on the phone and you need to say my name, say Boss. You tell Johnny and that crazy fucker Carson. We're in a new time, Bones." He hits his smoke again. "Now, get out of here."

I stand, walking to the door.

"And Bones," he says. I turn around at the nickname he's given me. "Don't ever do this again."

And I know he means it.

"Yeah," I reply lowly. I snatch open the door and walk out. "Johnny," I say. He and Carson get up from the couch they're occupying.

I see Nugget by the bar and walk over to him. "Yo, Nugget," I say. He turns to face me, and I rare back and punch him square in his fucking jaw.

"Goddammit, you little shit," he says, about to go after me.

Johnny grabs him. "You don't wanna do that. After all, Danny's Moretti's right hand."

"Bones," I correct him. "From now on, you'll call me Bones. And don't you ever point a gun at me again or, I swear to God, I'll blow your fucking brains out."

Nugget yanks from Johnny's hold. "Yeah, okay, Bones," he says acidly, reaching back for his beer. I lift my chin at Johnny and Carson and we exit the clubhouse.

"So, what's up with Bones?" Johnny asks.

"Moretti says we're in new times. We've got to be more careful on the phone." I look over at Carson. "You know anybody who cleans up better than Johnny?"

He shakes his head. "Nah. He's the best."

I smile. "Sweep fits you," I say to Johnny.

"I'll go with that," he replies.

"What the fuck you gonna call me?" Carson says.

I look down, knowing he's strapped. Crazy fucker is always ready to pull the trigger.

"Trig," I say. "We'll call you Trig."

He smiles.

"It's us three against the world." I grab my smokes from my front pocket as we climb into the car.

"So, what about Bexley?" Sweep says.

"What's done is done."

"No more of this getting out talk?" he asks me.

"Nah," I reply, lighting my smoke. I leave out everything that just happened back there and they don't ask about what I said to Nugget. "I belong here with you idiots." I lift my smoke as if it's a drink. "May the hinges of our friendship never grow rusty."

Trig laughs and hits the back of the seat. "We need a drink."

"I need a goddamn shower first. Take me to Ma's and then let's head to that little bar on the corner of Wimbish," I say to Sweep. "I think I saw a for sale sign. I might buy it."

Sweep starts the car, and we head down the road. Trig chatters about our future from the backseat, and Sweep looks ahead. I run my hand over my knotted necklace and remind myself that it's over and it's the best thing for both of us.

And maybe one day I'll believe it.

And maybe one day I'll take down Moretti because fuck him. I'll play this game for a while because I'm good at it. Because Bex is better off. But it won't always be like this.

One day I'll be free and I'm coming for her, and I'm going to end him.

Chapter Thirteen

Bones
2015

Yaps sits in the front seat of the car as Sweep drives us to the port. He's going on about some girl he was about to get with before Sweep asked him to come with us back at my bar a few hours after he was stuffing his face with olives.

"I appreciate you giving me this opportunity," he says, twisting back and looking at me.

"No problem," I reply with an easy shrug, looking over at Trig who shows no expression.

"Money's been tight lately and I've wanted to be in with you boys for a long time. So, what's the job, anyway?" Yaps asks. "What do you need me to do?"

"Relax. You'll see when we get there," I tell him.

He nods, but he's fidgety. He does too much cocaine and it makes me uneasy. Sweep pulls into the parking lot near the Hudson.

It's empty. Like always.

Insurgent

What was once supposed to be a nice place to take your family has been overrun by bums and monsters like me.

"What are we here for?" Yaps asks.

"You ask too many questions," I reply. "Let's go for a walk. The ship hasn't come in yet. I'll let you know the whole ins and outs of the business."

"Okay, sure. Sorry," he says, opening the car door as he sniffs, seeming a little less drunk than he was earlier. Cocaine will sober the drunkest motherfucker up. Sweep gets out and so do Trig and I. The river runs beside us as we walk. I look around again, making sure we are, in fact, alone. Most of the bums are probably standing in line to get in the shelter for the night.

"Our heroin business has grown tremendously over the last nine years. We're working with a Latin American by the name of Miguel, who works on a cargo ship transporting pure uncut China White from Latin America to the Jersey port near Postings.

"Sometimes we trade it for guns, so the insurgency can protect the farmers. Sometimes we pay money. It all depends on what we got and what they need."

Yaps nods excitedly. "Damn. This sounds like money."

I smile.

"Listen, Bones. I'm sorry about earlier. I crossed the line talking to you like that," he says.

"Sure, man," I reply, sliding my hand into my jacket's pocket as he and Sweep walk in front of us.

"I was out of line," Yaps says, sniffing, rubbing his fat stumpy fingers under his filthy nose. He looks back in front of him. I signal for Trig to back off.

"Yeah, you said that," I say to him. "You know, though, you do need to watch out for that. A man's mouth often breaks his nose."

"I know. I need to keep mine shut," Yaps says. "They don't call me Yapper for nothing." He laughs, and in one split second I pull out my gun and shoot Yaps in the back of the head. Sweep jumps to the side.

I chuckle. "Yeah, your big mouth is what got you killed, you disrespectful motherfucker." I spit on top of his dead body.

"Could have warned me," Sweep says with his hand over his heart.

"What? Did you think I would miss?"

Trig laughs. "You should see your face," he says to Sweep.

"Fuck you," Sweep says.

I pat him on the back. "I'd never shoot you. I gotta take a drive. Take care of this for me. I'll buy you a beer later."

"Where you headed?" Trig asks.

I wink. "Knowledge is power, my friend. Wouldn't you like to have it?" He rolls his eyes as

Insurgent

Sweep tosses me the keys. I grab a smoke from my pocket, lighting it as I walk to the car.

The night stretches farther than the light in this town as I ride through the south side. I look at the time on my watch. She should be closing up about now. I lean back, relaxing into the seat, thinking back on the day.

Per routine, my morning started with a run. I ran down into the neighborhood, passing by Ma's before turning the corner and going by the place where Sweep used to live.

Sometimes I can still smell the fumes. Moonshine, burning in the night, killing the bastard who used to beat Sweep. An aging Deputy Radcliff sits on the corner of the neighborhood, and like always, I give him a little wave as the sun starts to rise. He doesn't return it.

I think back on when he caught Bexley and me in the backseat of my car. I'd wanted her so bad that I could hardly stand it. I wanted to beat his face in for interrupting. He eats his donut and drinks his coffee like the good little crooked police officer he's always been. Like most of the cops around here.

I round the block a few more times, before I stop and head up to Ma's house. She's just turned eighty, still attends Mass loyally, and still plays bridge with her friends. She'll be up preparing breakfast, and if I had a million dollars, I'd bet Paul and Samuel are sitting at her table like they always do on Wednesday mornings.

I stop by just about every day, but we three make sure to meet up on Wednesdays and Sundays.

"There he is," Paul says as I walk into the dining room. He's in a tailored suit, reading the morning paper. He's old school that way.

"Morning," I say as Ma hands me a towel to wipe off with.

Samuel walks out of the kitchen with a plate of bacon.

"Brother." I nod at him as I slide a chair out.

"Danny," he replies.

I grab a cup from the middle of the table and pour myself some coffee.

"How's the family?" I ask Paul.

"Everybody's good," he says. *"Little Abby lost a tooth last night. The Tooth Fairy left ten dollars under her pillow."*

"Ten dollars?" Ma says. *"That's too much, Paul."*

"Well, kids these days," Paul says like that's the reason for it.

"Shit, I remember when we got a dollar."

"And that was too much," Ma says to Samuel. *"Don't put your elbows on the table,"* she scolds him.

He removes them with a smile, and I take a sip of my coffee.

"Come help me cook these eggs," she says to Samuel.

"Yes, ma'am," he replies, getting up. They both head into the kitchen and I'm grateful. I'd like to have a private conversation with my older brother.

"How's business?" I ask him.

"Fine," he says. "Trying to pass a new bill."

"Oh yeah? On what?"

He chuckles. "Nothing that benefits you."

I nod with a smirk.

"What about you, Danny? Or should I say Bones?" he says lowly.

I lick my lips, placing my cup on the table. "Business is better than ever."

"Really?" he asks.

"Really." I nod.

I link my fingers together, looking down at the tablecloth. Paul doesn't know too much about what I do. He knows enough, but it's better that he doesn't know details. In case someone questions him, he won't have to lie, even though he's great at it. He is a politician, after all.

"Well, don't beat around the bush, boy. Ask me what you wanna ask before they come back in here."

"Just want to make sure everything's quiet," I say, getting to the point. One thing about having a brother who's now the mayor of Postings is he has connections and he's friends with the DA.

He nods. *"I haven't heard anything concerning."*

"Good," I say.

"Can I ask you something?" he says, folding his newspaper.

"Go for it," I reply, grabbing a piece of bacon.

He straightens his tie. Paul's aged around the eyes. His hair's short, neat. His nails are manicured. We've come a long way from being shirtless in the streets, playing stick ball.

"When are you getting out of this shit? It's been some years now. Don't you want to start a family of your own?"

I chew my food slowly as I think on this. I tried to get out once, but I was foolish in thinking it would be as easy as walking into Moretti's office and telling him I was done. I only got a gun to my head for that. Now I'm so far in, it seems impossible to ever slip out.

"I could help, you know?"

I smile, knowing that's not likely. Moretti would find me, and he'd have too many people willing to help. I have enemies and he would use that against me. I have people who'd like nothing more than to see me six feet under, my eyes coinless.

You don't bend the law without getting blood on your hands. We're in the heroin trade and business is thriving; therefore, you have people who want a piece of it. When you're doing well, others want to *be involved. When you haven't got a pot to piss in, people seem to disappear. It's the way of the world.*

"Maybe one day," I say to Paul.

"You know she's happy now," he says. "It's time you were happy, too."

"I am happy."

"Are you, though?" My brother and I lock eyes, but we let that question go unanswered.

Samuel and Ma walk back. "Eggs are ready," Ma says. "Let's say grace."

I'm happy she didn't see me eating a piece of bacon already or I would have gotten a slap on the hand. We three bow our heads, hold hands, and Ma gets on with the blessing.

I smile to myself as I think about Paul's concern for me. It's always nice to sit with my family and share a meal, and it's nice to catch up with my brothers and hear Ma's laugh. I turn down the street that Bex works on and park the car just far enough so she can't see me.

I stare at the flower shop she's been at since she was in high school. It bothers me that she stayed there. She had so much talent with her photography. She could still be doing it for all I know, but no one has mentioned it. The lights go out in the shop, and moments later she steps out with keys in her hand and locks the door behind her.

Bexley has transformed into a gorgeous woman. She wears a pencil skirt, with a navy blouse and cream-colored heels. Her dark hair falls down her back, and I can't help but look at her ass when she walks to her SUV.

She climbs inside safely and heads home to another man. I sit in my car longer than I should before I head to my bar where I know Trig and Sweep will be.

The bar is lightly crowded tonight, and Mae, my bartender, gives me a smile when I walk in. I notice Trig and Sweep sitting at the bar watching a game. "Whiskey," I say as I take a seat beside them.

"She get home okay?" Trig asks.

I look over at him as Mae slides me my drink.

"Come on, Bones. You've got to stop doing this shit, man."

"Mind your business," I reply, taking a sip of my drink. "Everything get cleaned up?" I look at Sweep, referring to a dead Yaps.

He nods, not taking his eyes off the TV. "Got a problem at the warehouse, though."

"What's that?" I ask.

"We think one of the girls is stealing."

"How?"

"Not sure yet. But there's word about some overdoses. Someone's got to be cutting it with too much fentanyl and trying to sell it on the side."

"I'll pay a visit tonight. We can't let this shit slide."

He nods, grabbing a smoke from the bar as the door opens behind us. Samuel wears worn jeans and the same work boots he had on this morning.

"Haven't showered yet?" I ask him.

He laughs. "Long day. Can I get a drink, Mae?" he asks.

She nods, tapping her ringed fingers on the bar top. "Beer?"

"Please," he says.

"What brings you by?" I ask, taking a sip of my own drink.

"Got some news," he says, reaching for the beer when she places it down. He takes a big gulp and rubs his hands over his thighs.

I smirk. "Okay. Tell me this news."

He looks over at Sweep. "Johnny, you mind giving us a minute?"

Sweep exhales, clearly annoyed he's gotta take his eyes from the game. "Come on, Trig. Let's shoot a round." They get up and I watch my little brother as he bounces his knee. There was a time we couldn't even be in the same room without tension, but things have changed. I've accepted how life is now, even if it fucking kills me sometimes. And believe me, it does. My mind strays as I recall a time at Paul's house. It was a birthday party for one of his kids. Bexley was there and I couldn't take my eyes off her. She was in a sundress and her legs were tan. I wanted her so bad, I followed her out of the house when she slipped outside. I touched her thigh and I whispered in her ear. She wanted me, too, I could feel it.

"You talked to Paul?" Samuel asks, snapping me from my thoughts.

I nod, clearing my throat as I reach over, grabbing my smokes from the bar. "This morning, just like you did." I slide a cigarillo out. I stopped smoking cigarettes. Lost the taste for them years ago, but these right here are nice. I enjoy the flavor.

"Oh, right," Samuel says. "Still can't believe he's the mayor of Postings. He always said he would be. Surprised he still hangs around us."

I chuckle, slightly shaking my head as I hit my smoke. "Paul won't forget where he came from. We're all street kids. No matter where we go in life, that'll follow us."

My big brother has submerged himself into the political world. The college graduate moved to the nicer part of town and started hanging out with the bigwigs. He ran for mayor last year and won.

Of course, I threatened every motherfucker in this town, making sure they knew who they needed to vote for. Still, a win's a win in my book.

We all three went on different paths, but there's one thing we have in common. We work hard to get to where we want to be.

Insurgent

I place my smoke on the ashtray, lifting my glass of whiskey. "So, what's this news you've got? I know you didn't come here to talk about Paul."

Samuel takes another sip of his beer and exhales a quick, nervous breath as he looks at the bar. He then looks at me, pausing for a moment as his eyes study mine.

My smile fades.

"I'm going to ask Bexley to marry me."

My brows lift, and to be fucking honest, I feel like he just punched me in the gut.

"I know I'm not good enough for her," he says, looking at the label on his beer.

"None of us were good enough for her," I say. His eyes bounce back to mine as I lift my smoke, taking a heavy drag, darting my tongue out to my bottom lip.

He blinks, his eyes scanning my face. I scratch my five o'clock shadow and flick my ashes into the ashtray.

I want to hit him.

I want to pound my fist into my brother's fucking face until he doesn't exist anymore.

What a horrible person I am. Why did she have to pick him? Why didn't she move the hell away from Postings and do something with her life?

Samuel clears his throat. "I know you two always had this—"

"That's been over," I interrupt him. "We were just kids. What was once between us isn't anymore."

"Still, you two have a connection, Danny." He laughs, but it's humorless. "Truthfully, I think if you would have fought for her more, we wouldn't even be having this conversation."

My eyes dart to him for a moment, before I look at the TV hanging on the wall. *Fought for her more?* I went to jail because I fought for her so hard. I went to Moretti and tried to get out of this lifestyle for her, nearly getting myself killed.

I held her the night her mother died and fucked her any time she wanted. But none of that was good enough. Of course, he doesn't know any of that. He also doesn't know we met before they ever did. He doesn't know that Bexley Walker holds one of my biggest secrets.

She's a ghost in my life now. She visits me in my dreams. Sometimes I wake and I can smell her scent drifting in my room. The lake house is where I go to get away from time to time. It's filled with memoires of her, of us together. It keeps me in line, reminding me that one day things will be different.

I hit my cigarillo, the burning end sizzling lightly as it glows red. "She doesn't want me, brother. She's with the man she loves." I nod, exhaling smoke as I look over at him. "I'm happy for you." I'm not, though, and those words taste like acid, burning my throat, but like I said, she's made her choice.

"Thanks," he says as he lifts his beer. "I really didn't think this was going to go down this way."

"What way did you think it would go down? Me beating your face in until you choked on your own blood?" I ask.

He laughs, but then stops when he sees my expression. Oh, how serious I am right now, but I smile and nudge his arm. "I'm kidding, Samuel. Lighten up, man."

"Yeah, you seem like you're kidding," he replies, grabbing his beer. We don't talk for a moment, letting the chatter from the bar kill the awkward silence that would be here.

I'm a ticking time bomb. I feel the buzz in the back of my spine, crawling around my nerve endings.

"So, when are you going to do it?" I ask.

"Tomorrow night."

"All right," I reply, looking back at the TV. "All right."

I'm not a man who gets drunk very often. I'll have a drink or two, but I like to be alert. However, tonight is not one of those nights. It's late, and I'm the only one at the bar besides Mae. She walks from the back. I sit with a joint between my lips, looking over at her from the stool I occupy. Music drifts from the speakers. It's a slow tune.

"Dance with me," I say, sliding off the stool.

"You're drunk," she says.

"So?" I grab her, spinning her around. She laughs, her blonde dreads falling in front of her face. Mae's been my bartender for a long time now. We fuck when either of us gets a notion to. I never sleep with the girls at the clubhouse, so I go to her.

We sway to the music and she takes the joint from me, hitting it before she grabs my face and blows smoke into my mouth. My heart drops. I used to do this to Bexley when we were teenagers, riding around in my car and listening to music. I grab the joint and move away from her, tasting tequila and lime from her lips on mine.

I grab the bottle from the bar and tip it up.

She walks over to me, and grabbing the bottle, she takes a sip herself. She looks at me as she licks her bottom lip and I place the joint in the ashtray. I grab her by her neck and kiss her. She runs her fingers over my head, and I pick her up, quickly removing her shirt. I grab her breast and kiss her skin. She's braless and she moans when I suck her nipple.

Her hands go to my jeans and she undoes them. My mind wanders even now, in this moment, when

Insurgent

I should be thinking about the woman I'm with, I'm only thinking about the woman I want to be with. I slow my movements, my head falling into her neck. I breathe out and her head falls back.

"He's going to ask her, isn't he?" she says quietly, raising her head.

I lift my head, my eyes telling her the answer without me having to say it out loud. She told me this would happen. We've argued about it. I didn't want to believe it.

She nods, then clucks her tongue. "That's why you're drinking." She moves and I let her down.

"I won't let you make love to me and pretend like it's her. I won't let you treat me like that."

I turn around to face her, aware that my jeans are still undone. "I've never made love to you, Mae, and you know that."

She narrows her eyes at me, and I can tell I've hurt her. "You're a real piece of shit."

"I've never pretended to be anything different." She picks up the bottle and throws it at me, nearly hitting me in the head. Glass shatters. Liquor spills and she grabs her shirt, leaving me alone. I scoff, grabbing the joint from the bar and another bottle. I hit the joint, take a big gulp of whiskey, and then I fall to the floor. I lie there until daybreak and Mae comes back to find me passed out. I help her clean up, apologizing for the way I treated her, and then I go to my room and sleep until nightfall.

Chapter Fourteen

Bexley
One month three days missing

I startle when something wakes me. Blinking my eyes open, I rub them and quickly sit up on a gasp.

"It's just me," Danny says.

"How?" I ask. "How did you get out?"

"The ibuprofen made the swelling in my wrists go down. I recut them and was able to slide them through with my blood as a lubricant."

I flick my hair out of my face. "Jesus Christ, Danny," I say, standing up. "Let me look at them."

"They're fine."

"They're fine?" I ask sarcastically.

"Yes."

"Whatever."

"It's not like we can do anything about them anyway. No sense in worrying about me."

"I'm not worrying about you; I'm worrying about me. I don't want to be stuck here alone because you died from an infection before we could get out of here."

"Oh, and here I was thinking you were concerned for my sake."

"Why would I be?" I ask him. "You're the reason I'm in here. You're the reason…"

"You've said it before," he says. "Go ahead and say it again. I know you've been itching to for the past however many days we've been in this fucking place."

I look down.

"I'm the reason he's dead. There, I said it for you." He walks over to the stove, looking down at the dim burning fire.

"Do you even feel guilty?" I ask. "Or are you glad?"

His head whips around and he moves quickly for a man who's half-dead. I step back toward the wall as he towers over me. "You think I wanted him dead?" he asks.

I look him in the eyes. Danny's eyes have always been dark, just like his soul. But at one time, I did get to witness a speckle of light in them. When we were kids swept up in a fantasy that we could have a normal life together. When we thought love was enough.

But we grew up. I moved on because he moved on, and things just changed so much. We're not the same people anymore. Do I think Danny wanted *him* dead?

"Yes," I say.

His eyes bounce between mine. He breathes heavy, and from the moonlight I can see sweat on his brow. Tension builds, swarming around us like flies buzzing over a dead corpse. That's exactly how our love for one another is.

Dead.

We're both filthy, hurt physically and emotionally, and so damn tired, a week's worth of sleep wouldn't be enough.

"Maybe I did," he says, his shoulders dropping. "Does that make me evil?" he asks lowly, like he's scared to hear my answer, but at the same time he already knows.

"What happened to you?" I ask. "How did you sink so far in?"

"You happened to me," he replies, like that's all the answer there is.

I shake my head at him. "What a bullshit excuse." I move around him, clipping my shoulder with his arm.

"Why did you marry him?" he asks me. "Why did you even entertain the fucking idea?"

I look back at him. "I told you way. I loved him. You acted as if what Samuel and I had was nothing. You were wrong."

His back shutters as a breath leaves his lungs, like me saying those words cut him deeper than any knife could.

Good, he deserves it.

Chapter Fifteen

Bexley
2015

Resting the crate on my hip, I shut the trunk of my SUV and step over a puddle from the evening rain shower we just had. People walk by on the sidewalk; I nod and smile as I put the key into the lock and push open the door to A-Street Flower Shop. The small bell chimes above me, and the sweet aroma of fresh cut flowers and wisteria hanging on the charcoal walls fills my senses.

I did accept Billie's offer nearly nine years ago. I went home and talked it over with Uncle Hale, who at first didn't think it was a great idea. He wanted me to go off to college and meet new people, but I just never could leave.

I place the crate full of milk and eggs from Billie's farm on the black cement table that sits in the middle of the shop. It stretches down the center, filled with beautiful arranged flowers ready to be picked up by customers. You can also host dinner parties here. Lights are hung, zigzagging from one corner of the shop to the other. Evergreens are placed and hung throughout the shop, and in the back is a beautiful garden area with a fountain.

Billie did expand her shop, and we now have a whole side reserved for her vegetables and eggs and whatever else she grabs fresh from the farm that's in season. The local restaurant chefs stop by every morning and grab what they need if we have it.

Years have come and gone since Samuel and I started getting serious. It took me two years to give it a go with someone else, but I finally moved on. Samuel and I share a home together now, and he's helped me become the person I am today.

Danny fades in and out of my life. He shows up in short spurts. And even though I love Samuel, every time I see the man who only wears black, it's like a violent stab in the chest. My heart races and my mind scatters. I think back on the times we shared together. All the memories we have. That's the thing about memories. They're like a tattoo, forever inked onto your mind.

But we've grown up. We've moved on. We had a love that was too young. Doomed from the start. It's funny. Lately I find myself thinking about when we were kids. During that hard time, when Mama was dying and I stayed over at the O'Briens' house to keep my mind occupied from the reality of my childhood. My mama was leaving me, and neither one of us could do anything about it.

I don't think you can really ever get over a parent's death. You keep living your life, but the connection you felt to this world is untethered. It's just not the same.

But my chosen family helped me. They let me come into their lives, and they accepted me as one of them. But none of them seeped into my bones like Danny. Before we started a relationship when I came back, there were so many little moments that we had together.

"Grab some napkins, too," Paul calls out from the living room.

"Okay," I say, walking into the kitchen to get a few cans of pop for Paul, Samuel, and me.

The smell of hot pizza fills the house. Ma is out playing bridge with some of her friends. It's just the boys and me tonight. Except we're missing Danny, which is nothing new. I know later he'll come to my window, though, and I'll let him climb up the ladder he hides at the back of the house.

We've been doing this for the last year now. It just started one day and it hasn't stopped. Danny's visits keep my mind off the fact my mom's dying and soon everything will change for me. He tells me about the men he hangs out with, but he always seems to leave out certain things. I know the people he puts himself around aren't good men. I tell him that; however, he says they just have a different way of living. But when I rub my hand over his busted knuckles, I think maybe Danny's one of those men now.

I open the fridge door, looking for the drinks when I feel someone press against me from behind. I smell him, all boy and rough streets.

"Hey, Little Girl," he whispers in my ear, sending chills down my spine. Danny doesn't know it, but he's the reason I had my first orgasm. One night after he left my room, I lay on my bed smelling the pillow he'd just been on.

I don't know why his scent turned me on so much, but it did. My clit started throbbing and my hand had a mind of its on. I kept the pillow near my face and unbuttoned my jeans. Sliding my hand into my panties, I felt how wet I was, and as soon as my fingers rubbed over my clit, I felt a sensation that made tingles run down my thighs.

I kept rubbing until my toes curled and a rush of wetness filled my underwear, all the while thinking of Danny and his boyish smirk, his dark, unruly hair, and tan skin. For some reason, even the cuts on his damaged knuckles turned me on. I fantasized about his fingers rubbing me, his eyes focused on me and only me.

I shiver when he reaches around to move the milk, revealing the drinks. He grabs one and I turn around to face him.

"Where have you been?" I ask.

He shrugs. "Out." I look at his neck, seeing a hickey.

It hurts.

It literally causes my heart to shred a layer of skin, falling to the pit of my stomach like a drifting feather.

He smirks, noticing what I'm looking at. "Don't be jealous, Bexley."

Jealous? This isn't jealousy, you idiot. This is pain.

"Whatever," I reply with an eye roll. I always play it cool when it comes to Danny. I make him think I couldn't give a crap about him and his many girlfriends, but inside, I care enough to fill craters in the moon. Sometimes I wish I could just push him up against a wall and slap him and then kiss him crazy, but rejection is a hard pill to swallow and I just know he'd look at me like I was a little girl.

I turn back around, grabbing some drinks and a stack of napkins Ma keeps on the counter before I go back into the living room. I feel him follow behind me.

Samuel looks from me to him. "What?" I ask, giving him his drink.

"Nothing," Samuel says, his eyes going back to the TV. I sit down in the middle of the couch and Danny flops down beside me.

"Can I press play now?" Paul says, annoyed that I took so long.

Paige P. Horne

"Sorry," I mutter. With my heart in my stomach now, I don't want any pizza. Instead, I grab the blanket from the back of the couch and cover my legs before folding them so my feet dig into the cushion. I lay my head back as we start the movie, and only moments later Danny slides his hand under the throw, linking his fingers with mine.

I don't look his way, and I don't change my facial expression, but on the inside, I'm burning up and the happiest girl on the planet because Danny is holding my hand. Instinctively, I run my thumb over his knuckle, feeling the scab of a scar, and it brings me comfort.

I don't know why he held my hand that night. Maybe he felt bad for flaunting his hickey in my face. Maybe he just wanted to make sure I wasn't mad at him. Either way, I loved it, but he never did it again…not until much later, of course.

Danny stayed out more and more after that. He even stopped coming to my window, and when Mama died in the late summer of 1999, we shared one last moment together. He climbed into Paul's bed with me, he held me while I cried and after that I left Danny behind. We didn't speak again until Thanksgiving 2003. God, the time we had together. It was a hard rush. Every moment with him was electrifying and scary, and wild.

But it ended on a sad note.

Insurgent

And I know now that Danny and I are on two different paths. I'm supposed to be with Samuel.

He cherishes me. He spoils me and he makes me feel like I'm the most important person in his life.

I am completely content, and I might even say I'm happy.

There's just one thing missing.

I never can figure out what—I just know that there is. It wakes me up at night. Sometimes I watch the man I choose to live my life with sleep and I question things I shouldn't.

What if.

What if I would have forgiven Danny? What if I would have looked past everything he did and kept loving him no matter what? Would he be sleeping beside me instead of Samuel?

I shake my head, because I know even if I had Danny, I'd never truly have him. He's married to the streets. My bed would only hold me at night.

Samuel's a beautiful man. He's a hard worker, now the lead man of a construction crew.

I love him. I really do.

But there is nothing exciting about our life.

Walking over to the counter, I tilt my head when I see a note I didn't notice before.

Meet me in the alley. -D

My heartbeat soars and my throat becomes dry. With shaky fingers I fold the note and slide it into my trench coat's pocket. It's pathetic how fast I grab my keys and exit the shop. Jumping into my SUV, I crank it and hurry to the south side.

My mind races with things it shouldn't.

Why would he want to see me after all this time? Why wouldn't he just come to my shop and talk? He obviously knows where I work——slipping notes inside when I'm not there. What if Samuel had seen him? Anger replaces curiosity and I find myself mad at Danny, but then again, I'm always mad at him. Why has he never visited before now? Why not just call me like a normal person?

But Danny's never been normal. He's always been outside of the lines, on the wrong side of the tracks and mixed up in things he shouldn't be.

And the dark side of me loves every bit of it.

But the reasonable side of me rolls her eyes. You stupid woman. You point out the bad, only to replace it with an excuse.

"Ugh, I'm ridiculous."

Thirty minutes later, I pull into our old neighborhood. I head down the hill, rubbing a finger over my jaw as I remember the day Danny crashed into me.

And boy did he crash.

I roll past my old house, the one I lived in with Mama. The one I ran from when she left this earth, to seek comfort from a boy I had no idea would change my whole world.

Insurgent

I lift the locket around my neck that I've worn every day since I took it off my mama's. I press it to my lips and head on down the street to the alley I ran into the night she told me the cancer had spread.

Flipping down the visor, I run a finger under my eyes and pull up to the curb. I take in a deep breath and open the car door. Standing, I hold on to the edge of the door, looking around for any sign of Danny, and then I see a black car parked on the other side of the road.

The door opens and Danny climbs out the passenger side. I narrow my eyes as he adjusts his jacket and walks toward me. His chin is up, his eyes darting to me.

A black knight on his way to save no one.

I shut the car door, pulling my coat closer to shield my body from the cold wind. Danny walks past me and into the alley. I look at the car, seeing someone in the driver seat, but not making out who they are.

I look back at Danny just before he disappears into the alley. I follow behind him, and once both of the buildings surround me, Danny turns around.

His eyes drop down my body before he looks at my face. His hair is slicked back, shaved on the sides, his face scruffy. His clothes are all black, even the Tom Fords on his feet.

He's a dark god in an ominous alleyway.

The only skin not covered by ink is his face. It's pale from lack of sunshine and winter. Doesn't matter, though. He could be whiter than a ghost and still be breathtaking. Like a vampire, who's forever frozen in time, young and beautiful. Evil and pursuing his next prey. Danny's looks are steadfast.

"You look good, Bex," he says.

I narrow my eyes. "Why am I here?" I act like that compliment did nothing to me, but there's no denying the racing of my pulse.

"Because you want to be," he responds.

"I don't have time for games." Red-hot anger swims in my veins because this man hasn't bothered to come see me once. I see him at Christmas and Thanksgiving and maybe he shows up when one of Paul's kids has a birthday party.

Now, here we stand in an alley because he broke into the shop to leave a stupid note.

"Am I wrong? Would you have come if you didn't want to?"

I don't answer because the smug ass knows he's right. I would not have. I would have tossed the note into the trash and forgot about it, but that's the thing about Danny. I've never forgotten.

I cross my arms. "So, what do you want then?"

He narrows his eyes, not saying anything for a moment. He steps closer to the wall of one of the buildings we're between. Leaning back against it, like a dark shadow, he tilts his head to look at me.

"You happy?" he asks.

I blink. I was not expecting that. Am I happy?

"Define happy." I shouldn't have said that. I should have just said yes. Because I put doubt in his head and now he'll think I'm not.

He smiles, looking away before looking back. "Well, we all have a different definition of that, don't we?"

"I suppose." I uncross my arms, placing my hands in my coat's pockets instead. "I have a good life according to most people. A roof over my head, clothes on my back, yada, yada."

He smiles. "Yada, yada."

I taste the cold on my lips. "Are you happy?" I ask.

He sniffs, his eyes casting down. He pulls out a cigarillo and lights it. "Only if you are, love." Him calling me that…it kills me. It reminds me of times long ago. When we loved one another so fiercely. When he worshipped my body and I his.

I exhale, blowing a cloud of cold smoke into the evening air as Danny releases toxic smoke from his own lungs. The two gases drift up, mingling with one another. *How fitting*, I think to myself, and it's as if he thought it, too, because he nods and then he shocks me stupid.

"Samuel's going to ask you to marry him."

I feel my chest burn. "What?" I blurt. "How do you know that?"

"He came to the bar and told me I'm not sure if he was asking for my blessing. It would be the respectable thing to do, or if he just wanted me to know."

"Why would it be the respectable thing to do?"

He eyes me. "Why do you think?"

"I've been Samuel's for seven years now. So, I don't think anything."

He smirks. "Yeah. But are you his?"

"Are you asking if I'm not, or are you saying that I'm not?"

"I'm saying what we both know. That no matter where you lay your head, your heart will always belong to me."

I shake my head. "You're so sure of this, aren't you?"

"I'm more than sure." Leaning against the brick wall with his hand slid into his long wool coat's pockets, Danny looks like a gangster from the early 1900s. He puts the cigarillo between his lips, letting it hang there.

I grow angry at his cockiness and his indifference about mine and Samuel's relationship. He acts as if it's nothing. Meaningless.

I frown. "Why are you telling me this? Why have you asked me to come here so you can ruin an important time in my life?"

"Because, Bexley," he says in a way that sounds exhausted, "I want to know what you're going to say."

"Why does it matter to you what I say?"

Jesus Christ.

"It matters."

I link my fingers behind my head, looking up. Silence hangs heavy in the air.

"You said no to me so easily," he says.

I laugh. "We were kids. Stupid kids."

He nods, removing his smoke. "What if I asked you now?" He pushes from the wall, coming toward me. I freeze.

"What if I asked you to leave him. To marry me instead." He reaches up and puts a windblown hair behind my ear. "What would you say?"

My heart pounds, nearly jumping from my rib cage trying to get to his.

"Why are you doing this?"

"Because I love you. I've always loved you. I'd die for you."

I shake my head. "It's too late, Danny. It's too late for us."

"It's never too late."

"But it is."

He holds my face in his hand. "Tell me you don't want me. Tell me you don't think about me when you're with him."

I shut my eyes for a brief moment. "He's your brother."

"You were mine first," he says. "You were mine!" I jump. He moves his hand. "Don't you remember what we had together? Don't you remember what it was like? I knew you first."

He's killing me. He's ripping my heart out and crushing it. "We'll always have that, but my future isn't with you."

He turns away from me for a moment but then looks back, asking, "You in love with him?"

I take too long to answer. "I've always loved him." I cross my arms again, and his eyes jump to my wrist. Recognition flashes in them and his brow furrows, but he doesn't say anything.

He looks away from the bracelet he gave me when we were kids and there it is. That evil smirk only Danny O'Brien can pull off. "You can't lie to me, love."

"Danny, you know I love your brother. Don't be ridiculous."

"Oh, I know you love him. We all love him. But are you *in* love with him? Is he the man of your dreams, Bexley?" He steps closer to me. "Is he the guy you fantasize about when you come?"

"You motherfucker," I say slowly, my jaw tightening with anger. "How dare you. Yes, Samuel is the man of my dreams." I step even closer to him, lifting my chin so I can look right into his dark eyes.

"Not only is he the man I think about when I come, but he's the only one who makes me come."

I see the twitch in his eye, and I feel the energy rolling off of his body. "Really?" he says, his expression turning black. I know I'm being ridiculous, and now I'm just trying to hurt him, but how dare he come here and put me in this situation. How dare he ask me to choose.

"I've loved Samuel since I was a girl, and now I'll be his wife."

Stop it.

Fuck off, I reply to my conscience.

Danny may scare a lot of people, but he doesn't scare me.

He looks at me for a moment, his jaw ticking. "Fine," he says, but it's not convincing.

Wait.

What?

I expected more of a fight.

He hits his cigarillo, blowing smoke up into the air. My eyes go to the tattoos on his neck and hand.

He chuckles, his neck falling back more as he looks at the sky above us. "Fuck me." He hits his smoke again, opening his mouth and exhaling into the night.

Looking back at me with a frown camouflaged as a smile, he says, "Well, that's it then. You be happy. That's all I ever wanted." He points at me, letting his arm hang in the air for a short moment before he drops it to his side.

"Did you?" I ask, deadpan.

"Of course," he says. "Of course." He nods, looking off in the distance, and something... *acceptance?* washes over his face and it fucking terrifies me.

Panic sets in.

He nods once more as if coming to terms with his thoughts and then his eyes bounce to mine.

Fear wraps around my veins, running up the length of them as they flow to my heart.

He looks at me, *really* looks at me, making my mouth close and nerves swarm in my stomach. His eyes dart down my body, and then he says, "I'll see ya." He turns, flicking the smoke, and walks away from me.

Leaving me.

Again...

And like before, I do nothing.

Chapter Sixteen

Bexley
One month three days missing

"You loved him," Danny repeats the words I said. I did love Samuel, but I shouldn't have used that as a weapon to hurt Danny.

Still.

"Yes. I told you that. I never understood why you didn't believe me. Why else would I marry him, Danny?"

He turns around. "To hurt me. He was my brother, Bexley. My fucking blood and I had to watch you two together constantly. Do you have any idea how painful that was?"

I look down as my brow furrows.

"You honestly didn't think about it?" he asks. "How would you have felt in my shoes? To have the one person you love most in the world share a life with your sibling instead of you?" He walks over to the chair he's been sitting in for longer than any one person should. "How would you have reacted every time you witnessed that person smile and kiss another right in front of you?"

I don't say anything.

He lifts the chair only to slam it back down. "Tell me!"

I jump, my mouth falling open as I cross my arms.

His face turns deadly. He leans down with a slight wince. "How about I tell you," he says. "When my brother first came to me and told me he was going to ask you out, I saw red. I had to walk away from him to keep from hurting him. Did he ever tell you that?"

"No," I reply.

"He had some balls to do that."

"We'd been broken up for two years."

"Doesn't fucking matter if it was ten years. He broke a code."

I laugh. "A code?" I shake my head. "That's what he said to me the day you got hauled away in a police car. But he never elaborated on it. Tell me, what is this code?"

"That a man shouldn't go after his brother's girl, Bexley. Isn't it obvious?"

"Even if his brother's ex-girl could have a better life with that man? Didn't you tell me all those years ago that you just wanted me to be happy? So, I found happiness and here you are trying to make me feel guilty about it."

"You weren't happy. Even I know that. You were pretending to be happy. Pretending that having that little cookie-cutter life was what you wanted."

"Fuck you. You don't know anything about what I wanted."

"Oh, I don't?" he asks. "You want to stand here and act like you weren't completely happy when you were with me."

"I was an idiotic girl, Danny. Blinded by love to see the reality of our relationship and where it was going."

He nods. "Right. You'd rather be in a safe little bubble and live your life unsatisfied than be with a criminal." Sarcasm pours from his voice.

My hands start to shake, my pulse pounds. I step closer to him. "That's right. I didn't want to be with a criminal. So, I was alone for a while. I was sick, I was hardly living, and Samuel was there. He was always there, trying to bring me back to life. Where were you, huh?" I shove him. He winces. I feel bad, but I don't stop. "Off murdering someone because they were a threat to your livelihood? Fucking the next whore at the clubhouse?

"You stand there and throw judgment at me for trying to move on from you. For trying to live my life with half a heart…" My voice cracks and my hand goes over my mouth to keep the sob from being heard. I've been strong for so long when it comes to Danny. I've told myself over and over that the life I chose was far better than the life I would have had with this man.

But love is love and I can't shake it.

I just can't shake it.

Samuel was everything and more. He deserved the world, and I could only give him a small piece of me because the man standing here owned almost all.

"I was living half-brokenhearted when I was with you. Waiting for you to mess up."

"That was your problem," he says. "You always thought the worst of me."

"You showed me the worst. What else was I supposed to believe?"

He grows angry. "That I loved you! That I was trying."

"You were trying?" I laugh, wiping my tears. "Tell me how you were trying?"

"I didn't mean to not show up!"

"Oh, that's right. You hit a deer," I say sarcastically.

His jaw clenches.

"How about you tell me some truth? Tell me what really happened all those years ago."

Chapter Seventeen

Bones
One month three days missing

She stands there crying and I'm shaking. Shaking with rage, with hurt, with a heart so full of love only for her. I haven't felt much in a long time. My soul faded to black a long time ago, but listening to her cry as she tries not to, it breaks something inside of me.

"I'm sorry," I say, shaking my head and gripping the chair. "I'm not being fair."

"Well, you never were," she replies, wiping at her face.

"No, not when it came to you, I guess I wasn't." I run my hand over my beard, happy to be able to move my damn hands. Such a simple thing we take for granted…moving our hands.

Jesus.

I'm still fucked up from finding out it's Trig. I'm heartbroken about it.

This is going to sound shitty—fuck, what do I care? I'm more torn up about Trig than Samuel. Because to me they're both gone. But the fact that he's done this to us…

God help him.

"Are you going to tell me?" she says.

"You really want to know?"

"Yes."

I nod. "We were heading back from a moonshine run. Moretti was selling it to the liquor stores for more than he paid. He was making a good profit; therefore, we were making good money. I noticed someone following us, so Mickey, Moretti's right-hand man at the time, told me to pull over. Turns out, it was some meth heads, fucked up off their ass. They were trying to rob us. Things went south. They shot Mickey. He died on the way home."

"The blood on you that night?" she questions. "It wasn't from a deer then."

"No. I lied. It was Mickey's. We buried him."

She shakes her head. "Why do you do this? Why do you want to live your life like this? I'll never understand it. We could have had it all together."

"But you said no," I remind her. "Twice."

Chapter Eighteen

Bones
2015

I leave her in the alley, her words soaking through my skin. *"I've loved Samuel since I was a girl, and now I'll be his wife."*

I've known Samuel was in love with Bex, but shit, I didn't think she felt the same way. I mean, they've been together for years now, but part of me always thought...fuck, I don't know what I thought.

She's always looked out of place on this side of town. Too good for it, maybe, but now, damn. She's otherworldly. The way she carries herself, the way she dresses like she just stepped out of a goddamn board meeting with some big CEO.

She's still wearing the bracelet I bought her all those years ago, and that does something to me.

I head back to my car, climbing into the passenger seat.

Sweep looks over at me.

"What?" I say.

"The fuck you doing, Bones?"

"The fuck you mean, Sweep?" I ask. "Start the car. Let's go. It's done."

"Yeah, I'll believe that when one of you is below ground," he says exasperatedly. He shakes his head slightly. Putting the car into drive, he heads down the road.

Sweep looks at me for a moment too long but doesn't say anything farther. The sun has faded now, the night taking over. It makes my soul happy. I feel at home in the dark, because I'm a monster and monsters feed off it.

I look out the window, thinking about Bexley and wondering how she's going to react to my brother asking her to marry him.

Maybe she'll put on a happy smile and act surprised. Maybe she'll be a fool and tell him that I already told her.

Before today, I hadn't been in that shop in years. I always ride by in the evening—when the sun is fading, and I know she's closing up—just to make sure she's okay.

Just looking at her helps settle me down at night. She's my shot of whiskey; she soothes me. I do a lot of shit. I hurt people, and she helps me remember that one day I won't.

"Head to the warehouse. I need to check on this little thief."

"You know you have to move on from her eventually, right?"

"Yeah, well, she's marrying Samuel, so what better time?"

Sweep looks over at me. "Did you tell her?" he asks.

"I did."

"Damn, brother."

"I had to. I asked her to marry me, too."

"You're fucked in the head," he says. "You fucked up his proposal and you tried to steal her away from him."

"The hell you care if I fucked up his proposal?"

"He's your brother, Bones."

I laugh. "And he's marrying the woman I love. Ain't that some shit?" We pull down the road, nearing the warehouse.

"That's life at its finest," he replies. We stop the car and Trig walks out the side door that Daryl and Sip stand by with black suits and guns under their blazers. Two men guard every door leading into the place.

He lifts his chin at Sweep, reaching his hand out for mine. I return it. "I know who it is," he says, after our shake, sliding his hands into his pockets. "Been looking at the tapes with Nugget. She's been doing it for a while."

"How have we not seen this?" I ask.

He shakes his head. "Someone wasn't doing their job, Bones."

I nod. "Well, let's find out who that someone is and get the girl."

"Yes, sir," he says. We head toward the door and Sip and Daryl nod firmly at me.

"Boys," I say. "Daryl, your grandma still baking those homemade red velvet cakes?"

"Yes, sir," he says, "Believe she just finished baking some today."

I nod. "Think she'll have an extra to sell?"

"For you, I'm sure," he says.

"Great. I'm sure Ma would love a slice. It's her favorite." He nods and Sip opens the door for us. Naked women, lined in rows, cut the heroin, scoop the powder into baggies, weigh them. and continue the process.

"How is she doing it when they have no fucking clothes on?" I ask Sweep.

"Someone had to be helping," he says.

"You think?" I reply. He eyeballs me. I lift a brow. "Come on, let's go take care of this shit. Mae's making pot roast for supper and I don't want to be late."

"She's cooking for you now?" he asks.

"She works for me, Sweep. Drop it."

"You paying her to fuck you, too?" Trig asks.

"Can I ask how the hell that's any of your business? Jesus Christ, Trig. I don't keep up with who you fuck. Mind your own shit." I reach up and pop him on the back of the head.

He chuckles. "Girl's back here," he says. We walk to her row. I watch her for a moment as she works. She's thin, her ribs stick out, and her hipbones have no meat.

But her ass is nice, and her boobs have that perfect droop, a handful's worth. "Grab her."

Trig walks over and snatches her by the arm. Her titties bounce, and her bare feet slide on the cement floor. The other girls shift around her.

"All right, back to work," I say as Trig walks on with Sweep right beside us.

"What's going on?" the girl asks.

"You tell us?" Trig says, gripping her arm tightly. He shoves her into the office and Sweep shuts the door.

"Have a seat," I tell her. Walking over to the desk chair, I grab the button-down shirt off the back and toss it to her.

"Put this on."

She quickly slides her arms through and pulls the front across her body instead of buttoning it.

I flip the TV on. "Show us," I say to Trig.

He takes the remote and fast-forwards the tape. And that's when I see her take a baggy and place it under her arm. It's enough to where if she mixed it heavily, she'd be able to sell a shitload, plus how many times has she done this?

"Who's working with you?" I ask, knowing the men check the women before they leave the warehouse.

She swallows.

"It's better for you if you tell me now." I take a seat on the edge of the desk, grabbing my cigarillos from a box. I snap my fingers at Sweep, and he tosses me his family heirloom. I flip the Zippo open and light my smoke.

"You know how Sweep got this?" I ask the girl.

She shakes her head and I see the tremble in her lip.

She's scared.

She should be.

I run my finger over the scratched silver. "It was his father's. But you see, Sweep didn't have the type of dad who would pass this sort of thing down. Sweep's dad used to burn him with the cigarettes he lit with this." I stand up, bending down in front of her. I grab her arm, making her grip loosen on the fabric of my shirt. "Open your hand."

She listens and I flip it over so her palm is facing down. "Know what we did to Sweep's pops?"

Her fingers start to shake.

"Do you know what skin smells like when it's burning?"

Her eyes grow wide.

"Tell me," I say softly. "Who's working with you?" I tilt my head slightly, looking over her face. She's got a scar above her lip; it reminds me of the scar on Bexley's jawline. I reach up, running my finger over it.

And then I grip her wrist tight, striking the Zippo.

She starts to whimper. "Sweep's pops never saw it coming. He was asleep, passed out from drinking too much. He always did that, didn't he, Sweep?"

The big man nods.

"All you gotta do is say a name."

She pulls at her arm.

"Trig," I say. He walks over, holding her in place. I bring the flame closer to her open hand. "We didn't get to hear him suffer, but maybe hearing you will make up for that."

The flame sits just below her skin and she starts to cry out, moving frantically.

I move it closer, and she screams as it starts to burn her skin.

"One name," I say.

"Daryl," she says. "It's Daryl!" I flip the lighter closed and stand up.

I nod, running a hand through my hair after I toss Sweep back his lighter. "Get rid of her," I say to Trig.

"No, I won't tell anyone," she begs.

"You knew the risk when you took a chance on fucking me over, sweetheart."

Trig lifts her over his shoulder, carrying her out of the office.

"Go get Daryl," I say to Sweep. "He and Sip seem to be best buds. Sip will kill him."

Chapter Nineteen

Bexley
One month three days missing

"You know why I said no to marrying you, right?" I say.

"No."

I exhale. "Seriously, Danny. Both proposals were shit."

"So, if I did the whole flowers and romance thing, you would have said yes?" he asks doubtfully.

"No. You picked very crappy timing."

"So, if my timing was better?"

I shrug with a smirk. "Maybe."

He scoffs. "I need a drink and a smoke." He gives me a smile, though, and it slays me. I walk over to where he's standing by the window. He's leaning back against it, and as I walk near him, he watches me. I copy the way he stands. Our hands are close, our fingers only inches from one another. He smells like pine and dirt, but for some reason, it makes my mouth water. I miss him.

"Why did you tell me Samuel was going to ask me to marry him?" I don't know why I ask this question. I'm only ripping a scab off, but part of me really needs to know.

He runs a hand over his beard, looking at me in the darkness, save for the fire in the stove and the moonlight coming in through the windows. It would be romantic if we weren't filthy and being held against our will.

"I guess part of me thought you wouldn't say yes," he says as a piece of log pops.

"You thought I wouldn't marry him?" I ask.

"That's what I said."

I roll my eyes. "You're so self-assured, aren't you? So goddamn cocky. You thought that I would turn him down, and what? Run back to you?"

"Yes. You were never supposed to marry him, Bex."

I shake my head, because this man is so unbelievable. He really has it set in his mind that we were meant to be together.

Is he wrong?

"Right. I was supposed to marry you. What did you want me to do, put on my black gown and run off with you into the pits of Hell?"

He narrows his eyes. "If not me, then you should have gotten out of this fucking town and did something with your life."

"I did do something with my life!"

"You work at a flower shop. That's not you. That's not what you were meant to do."

"I'm so goddamn sick of you thinking you know what's best for me."

"Why wouldn't I? I know you better than anyone. I know you better than you know yourself."

"God, you are a piece of work, Danny O'Brien. How have we not killed one another by now?"

"I'd never hurt you."

I laugh. "You hurt me the most."

He doesn't laugh.

Chapter Twenty

Bexley
2015

I exhale as I pull up to the curb of our house. Samuel's truck is here, but there isn't a single light on in the place. We have a white picket fence that surrounds the yard with a small gate. The sidewalk goes up the middle to the beautiful porch Samuel expanded around the house. Evergreens hang from above, and there's seating on every side.

Our front door is big and crimson. Our shudders are black, and the house is a magnificent white. Samuel and I worked hard on this home. We've made it our own and I absolutely adore living here.

I swallow, nerves swarming in my stomach. I grip the steering wheel. I don't know when he's going to ask me, but I do know I will say yes to marrying Samuel. I love him. We have a nice life that most people would kill for.

I will let go of my past, and I will focus on my future. I study the yard as the moon shines down on it. I picture kids running around, jumping through a water sprinkler and a dog chasing behind them.

That's a good life.

I exhale, giving the night a nod.

This is it.

This will be it.

Once I agree to marry Samuel, I will shut off my feelings for Danny. I will let him go, because I've chosen my path and he's chosen his and neither one of us fits on the others.

It's as simple as that.

With that affirmation, I shut the car off and get out. I grab a fresh bouquet that I put together at the shop after I left Danny in the alley and head inside.

My tan trench coat hits the back of my black stockings as my heels tap against the sidewalk. I take a step onto the porch, and that's when I see a flicker of fire in the living room. I open the door that's already unlocked and the hand with my keys in it goes to my mouth as I hold on to the flowers.

My eyes scan over every inch of this place covered in burning candles, and not just any candles, but my favorite—frosted cranberry. The fireplace is going, and I hear music coming from the radio. I walk over to the couch, sliding over a candle or two so I can put the flowers down. I remove my coat, straightening out the sleeves on my hunter green dress.

"Samuel?" I call out.

"Hey, Bex."

I twist around when I see him standing near the hall that leads to the kitchen. He leans against the white shiplap. His arms are crossed, his feet bare.

Samuel wears worn jeans and no shirt. His skin is still tan from working outside all summer. His chest is defined, his arms perfect. Samuel's veins twitch under his forearm and he has no idea how hot I think that is.

Especially when he's on top of me.

He's a beautiful man inside and out.

"What's all this?" I ask with a smile, trying not to let the conversation I had with Danny ruin anything.

He licks his full lips, his eyes dancing over the place before they go back to me. And when he looks at me, he truly studies. Samuel has always had a way of *seeing* me.

But not what I hide behind a cemented wall. Not the ugly side that he surely would not recognize. The side that loves his brother. She wears black, too, with dark crimson lipstick and thigh-high boots, and when she was a kid, she threw rocks at windows and broke into the school to fuck with the teachers' things.

She swiped candy at the convenient store just because Danny told her to and skipped school so she could sneak into the movies with him and eat popcorn that he had the money for because he "mowed lawns". *At least that's how he told me he got the money.*

She let that boy crawl into bed with her because she was sad about losing her mom, and after that night, she dreamed of him often, waking up with soaked panties and a pounding heart.

But she's no longer allowed to come out. Now the side that arranges flowers is all the world sees. She dresses well and is a good model citizen. She helps out in her community, giving back to children with no parents. She's grown up a lot, but sometimes she misses the girl she used to be.

Life has a way of molding you. Shaping you into what society thinks you should be. I guess that's what attracted me to Danny.

He gives no fucks.

He throws up his middle finger to society and its fucking rules.

But I realize you can't go on like that. You have to be a part of society and understand that there are rules.

And here I am thinking about Danny when I have a beautiful man standing in front of me...most likely about to ask me to marry him.

A man I am lucky to have. Samuel is the one who watched a movie with me when I lost my mom and was heartbroken. He's the one who carried my books when we first saw each other again in the halls after years apart.

I love the special attention he gives and the fact that he listens to the hopes and dreams I have. Not only listens, but makes them a reality. Any girl can want a white picket fence, but actually finding a man who gives you that…well, that's special.

Samuel pushes off the wall, walking closer to me.

"The first time I saw you, you were in a flowery bathing suit with water raining down on you. The sun was shining through the water, giving off this halo effect. I was just a kid, but I thought there's something extraordinary about this girl."

I swallow as Samuel stands in front of me, my eyes going to the hair on his chest.

"And then you started coming over all the time. I watched you laugh with Paul and roll your eyes at Danny's indifference. But the thing I watched the most was how you looked at me. You were my friend first. You listened when I talked and spent time with me. You cared about my baseball games and whatever else I had going on."

I loved watching Samuel play baseball. He was a natural. Still is when the boys from his work get together. I guess we both *see* each other, and maybe that's why we work.

"I believe running into you all those years ago and then prom working out the way it did…I think it was fate. I know that life is going to be hard sometimes. I know that we will have our struggles. But I believe for two people to have a successful relationship, they both have to decide that no matter what battles they face, they'll suit up together.

"I want to fight every war beside you, Bexley. I love you."

With the candle flames dancing across our walls and reflecting in his eyes, Samuel goes to one knee. My heart jumps, my eyes water, and there are the butterflies. Those beautiful winged creatures soar with purpose, reminding me why I fell in love with this man. It's because he's always been there.

He's shown up every time.

That goes past lust and want.

Being there for someone is love without telling.

He opens his hand. "I was going to wait to do this, but something told me to go ahead." He smiles. "Will you marry me?"

A ring with a single diamond sits in a black velvet box in a hand that's loved me, built this home, and made a life for us. My heart beats happy; my soul breathes.

The girl who hides inside of me weeps because she knows that once we make this choice, that's all there is.

My knees bend and I sink to the floor with him. He watches me. I reach out and run my finger down the side of his handsome face, giving him a small smile. I adore this person.

I adored the boy he used to be and the beautiful man he is today.

"Yes, Samuel." A tear runs down my face and not because I'm overjoyed with happiness, but because my heart is breaking in two.

I'm choosing.

"I will marry you."

He smiles and grabs my face, kissing me with such emotion, it knocks the air from my lungs. He reaches around and unzips my dress. I grab the front of his jeans and undo the button before pulling the zipper down. Samuel treats me like glass, and I'm not sure if it's because he really thinks I'm that fragile or he's afraid if I break I'll slice him in two.

———————————

Staring at the clock on my bedside table, I decide sleep isn't going to come easy tonight. Looking over at Samuel sleeping on his back with his hand resting on his stomach, I quietly slip out of bed. Grabbing my thick knitted cream sweater from the end of the bed, I tiptoe out of the room. Walking into our kitchen, I pour myself a stiff drink before I head into the living room. The fire is out, the candles, too, but the smell of cranberries still drifts in the air. I snatch a throw from the couch before I slip outside.

The night air is crisp, making my nipples pucker beneath my silk tank. I wrap the sweater around me tighter. The outdoor sofa creaks when I take a seat and cross my legs so I can cover up my feet and legs.

With a heavy sigh, I look out at the road, taking a sip of my drink. The liquor warms me from the inside as my eyes land on a black car and the outline of a man leaning against it.

He brings a cigarillo to his lips, the end burning crimson as he hits it. I see him look up and a thick fog of smoke blows from his mouth into the night air. I look up, too, watching as the smoke dances into oblivion. My finger plays with the new ring on my hand.

So much could be said, but it seems neither of us will say anything. I look back at him, my heart in my throat. If this were a different lifetime…God, if he was a different man and not married to the lifestyle he's chosen. If I were gullible to the ways of the world and I hadn't started a life with Samuel, I'd stand and walk out to him.

In my mind, I imagine how it would go. How the cold porch steps would feel against my bare feet as I took them one at a time. How he'd realize I didn't have on shoes, so he'd come to me, scowling me for being out in the cold, like I was still a little girl.

I'd roll my eyes but get back to the porch anyway, knowing he'd follow.

"Why don't you have on shoes?" he questions.

I hurry and sit back on the sofa, covering my chilled feet with the throw. "I didn't think I'd be walking."

"Why did you?" he asks, walking up the steps.

"You were there," I reply, like that's all there is.

"So, because I was standing there, you decided to get pneumonia?" He smiles as he hits his smoke, looking dangerous in the night, but also looking more at home because of it.

"Don't be so full of yourself," I say, gripping onto my toes under the blanket.

Danny stands near the porch railing with Cole Haan oxfords on his feet, black with a white rim around the bottom. Black jeans cover his legs, and he wears a black shirt. The zippers on his jacket shine in the night. He makes black look like sin. Delicious and tempting.

"Wanna come in?" I ask.

"You sure about that?" he questions with a lifted brow.

"Yes," I reply, standing. I walk to the door, knowing he'll follow. I walk inside, tossing the blanket onto the couch as the door clicks shut.

I'm officially going to Hell, because I just invited the devil in.

"Want something to drink?" I ask.

"No," he says, looking around the house. He's seeing it for the first time, and I like watching that.

"Danny," I say, getting his attention. He looks over at me. "Why are we doing this?"

"Because it's all we know," he answers.

"I'm tired."

He looks to the floor and then back at me. "Come here," he says, his head slightly tilted.

My feet move gently across the floor, almost like I'm floating. I stand near him now, so close yet still too far.

He makes my chest cave, the way he looks at me. It's like he's seeing the universe for the first time, with all its trillions of stars and mysterious planets.

"Choose me," he says, his voice filled with deep emotion.

The muscle that keeps my body alive bursts into tears. "'Do you know how long we've wanted to hear those words?'" it says to his own heart.

"Don't you see, Danny?" I shake my head, my eyes going to his lips. "I never had a choice." I look back at his eyes. "It's always been you," I whisper.

Lips have never crashed so hard. Want has never been so fierce. Lust gets jealous and love runs.

His hands claim me, like they should for all these years. His soul reaches for mine, breaking through flesh to succeed in its mission.

I'm lifted onto the table behind the couch, happily spreading my legs so he can slide between...

Insurgent

A car door shuts, snapping me back into reality, and I see the truth of our life. I'm marrying Samuel, and Danny's driving by, and I have this sick feeling that I won't be seeing him for a while. But I had that same feeling earlier when he told me goodbye.

Oh, well. What's done is done.

I take in a deep breath, leave the sofa, and walk back inside, happy and devastated at the same time.

Chapter Twenty-One

Bones
One month three days missing

It pains me for her to say I hurt her the most. But I'm not blind to that. I know I've hurt her. We've hurt each other. It seems to be a habit now. A bad one.

"That was never my intention," I say to her. My voice is low.

"Still," she says.

"Yeah." I nod.

"You know he asked me that night," she says. "The night you told me."

"I didn't."

She runs her finger over her wedding ring. "It was very romantic. He had candles—"

"I don't want to hear it," I interrupt her.

"I get that, but you know what stands out the most about that night?"

"What?"

"You."

"Me?"

"Yes, you. You stood outside in the dark and watched me."

I don't say anything. I remember her sitting out on the porch. It was cold. I just needed to be near her.

"Why did you come by?"

"I don't know," I lie.

"I was glad," she says.

"Why?" I look over at her. The moonlight reflects blue against her pretty face. I should have fought harder for us. I want to kiss her now, but I'm afraid it's too soon.

"I don't know."

I exhale, looking away so I won't be tempted any longer.

"You didn't come to the wedding," she says.

"I was busy."

"Right," she replies, like she understands what I'm not saying.

Of course, I didn't attend the wedding. How could I watch that? After they were married, I faded away into the dark world I chose to live in. I kept an eye on Moretti and I did what was natural to me and I started to be okay.

Chapter Twenty-Two

Bones
2019

I tap my foot to the beat of the music as I sit back on my couch with a lit joint between my fingers. Norman Greenbaum croons about spirits in the sky as his record spins on my record player. Bringing the weed to my lips, I think about past days.

That little gem, time, has changed several things over these last four years. The more days that pass, the more sins we commit. The more weight gets stacked on top of our shoulders.

My brother and Bexley were married a few months after their engagement and that was that.

I started traveling a lot with the boys, throwing myself into this lifestyle. I've done things over these last few years that can't be forgiven, but let's face it, I've been doing inexcusable shit all my life.

In the back of my mind, I've always known who I am. Known who I wanted to be.

On top, in charge of my own. I have that now.

She's with him.

I'm married to the streets.

A few months back, we headed to Atlanta to meet up with the cocaine man Mickey was working with before he died. He was right when he said he was crazy as hell. The man, Simon, has a fucking tiger in his backyard. Every time we go down there, he's always playing his music so loud you can hardly think, and it's eighties shit. Simon has a pile of cocaine sitting on his bar, like olives ready to be plucked from a dish.

Trig took advantage of that and got fucked up. He started shooting his gun off in the goddamn house. It was a shit show. But we ended up working out a deal, and now we make runs there once a month.

There's this club down there called Red. It's something else, man. Huge gambling business going on below it. Unfortunately, we ran into a little cheating issue and had to handle it accordingly. Nothing worse than a fucking cheater.

An old friend of Sweep's and mine from church does security work for the man who owns the place.

Bryce Grant is the owner's name.

He's impressive. Started the place from the ground up and turned it into a moneymaker. Sadly, all good things must come to an end. Moretti got word that Bryce was about to get busted and he saw the perfect opportunity for us to sweep in and take it.

Moretti called me into his office.

"Kid's no older than you and making more money than Elon Musk."

"I know," I say, sitting back in the brown leather chair, enjoying a glass of bourbon and a cigar. Moretti's got gold rings on his fingers and a belly rounder than that purple girl from...what's that fucking movie? Charlie and the Chocolate Factory. *Yeah, that's the one. Because all his fat ass does is eat, shit, and fuck.*

He's lazy and it bothers me.

"I want a piece of it," he says.

"That why you called me in here?" I ask. I never mentioned getting out again after he let Nugget put a gun to my head. I've made him a shitload of money and I've made myself a shitload of money. And I've watched. Everything. Carefully.

"Yeah. I know you can make that happen. The boy's going to get caught. Too many people talking about it now. Plus, I got word that some cunt from the FBI agency is investigating him."

I lift a brow as I hit my cigar. This room is dark, nothing but two small lamps on. Outside of this office is the clubhouse. The boys have strippers tonight and the music vibrates the walls. I look to the door when someone taps on it before walking in.

"Hey, I'm fucking busy here," Moretti yells at the girl who I recognize. She's one of his. She's been working for him for years and it shows.

Moretti's got his hand dipped in everything these days.

He's greedy.

And greedy people get careless.

"Sorry, boss," she says before she slips back out. Too much makeup, yet not enough to cover the telltale sign she's been used up.

Moretti sits back in his chair, looking at me for a beat. "You need to enjoy life more."

"I enjoy life," I reply, tasting the cigar on my lips.

"The hell you do. You're always so uptight. So goddamn serious."

My eyes shoot over to him. "Should I not be?"

He shrugs. "You're cold, Bones."

I look back in front of me. "Yeah, well, life will do that to you." I reach up and tap my cigar against the glass ashtray.

He laughs. "This life will." Moretti sits up and links his chubby fingers together. "You were born for this shit. I saw it in you when you were just a boy. The day you came to me and told me you wanted out." He tilts his head, squinting his eyes. "You broke my heart. After all I did for you and you came at me with that shit. You know I could have ended you right then. You know Nugget has been itching to do that since you grew hair on your balls."

I keep my expression bleak, but on the inside, bats are swarming, blood is pumping, and my dark soul is simmering. I once had mad respect for this man, but over the years that has faltered.

He sits back, laughing. "Relax, Bones. I'm just yanking your chain here."

I shrug. "Who says I'm not relaxed?"

He nods. "Well, let's get to work. Get down to Atlanta and make this happen."

Mae walks out of the bathroom, grabbing a hair tie from her arm, snapping me from my thoughts. I exhale as I sit up, running a hand over my bare chest, lifting my necklace as I hit the joint. Ashes fall, and I move my leg, letting them hit the floor.

She lifts her dress from the carpet and slides it over her head before grabbing her heels near the bed. "See you downstairs."

I lift my chin as she exits my apartment above the bar I own. I haven't been home for some time now. After Moretti and I had that conversation, I headed to Atlanta. I hung around for a bit and learned all about Bryce's setup and I watched from afar as the FBI watched him.

Moretti handed me a dump truck full of money to go down there and try to purchase Red so he could have a stable place to run his drugs in the South. Plus, the gambling business is a moneymaker, and that club is the best Atlanta has to offer.

It wasn't long before Bryce did get busted and I took my chance. You see, I know people, my brother being the mayor and all. So, I worked it out, that if Bryce let me buy the club from him, I'd get him out of his sticky situation, which was some serious time.

Don't get me wrong. I like the guy and I don't like many people, but I'm about business first.

I knew he had a girl he cared about, so I, of course, brought her up. I was simply trying to make him see what he had to lose if he chose not to sell.

But Bryce is a smart man. He didn't get to be successful because of luck and he chose right. He's now a free man, and Moretti owns Red.

I go down and check on things for him and get a cut of the money coming out of there.

It's a win-win for us all.

I put the joint out, smoke exhaling from my mouth as I stand up, popping my neck before I walk over to my closet. I grab a black button-down shirt and put it on, taking a seat on my bed as I lean down and slip my feet into some rustic brown dress boots.

Sitting up, I run a hand through my hair. I stand, snatching my black blazer from the back of my chair, slipping it through my arms. I spray myself with cologne, stop the record player, and head out.

Jogging down the stairs, I look and see Trig and Sweep sitting at the bar. It's early, but we still have the same drunks we always do.

Don't matter the time for an alcoholic. It could be ten a.m. or ten p.m. A drink is needed either way for them.

"Boys," I say to Sweep and Trig, rubbing my hands together. "We're going to church. It's been a while."

They both look at each other.

"Come on," I say. "It's time we go confess some of our sins."

"They'll throw us out, Bones," Trig says.

Sweep flicks his Zippo and chuckles and the motherfucker never does that. He hardly even smiles.

"Let's go anyway. Mae, get me a cup of coffee, would you?" I ask as Trig and Sweep stand up. "Ma will be glad to see us there."

"What the hell's gotten into you?" Trig asks.

I smirk. "I'm in a good mood. Don't kill it." I grab the coffee mug. "Hurry. We'll be late."

Chapter Twenty-Three

Bexley
One month three days missing

"Was Samuel good to you?" Danny asks. We're still standing side by side. The fire is still burning in the stove, filling the room with warmth and a smoky scent.

"Yes, he was." Samuel was always good to me. Was I good to him? No. I loved him, I did, but he didn't have all of me like I had all of him, and that wasn't fair.

But I'm learning life isn't fair. You get what you get sometimes even if you deserve better.

"I never doubted he would. As much as I hated you two being together, I did know he'd treat you well."

"Why ask then?" I say.

"It's never a bad idea to get confirmation."

"I get that. We did have our problems, though."

"I remember," he says.

I narrow my eyes. "You remember what?"

"That time we all met up at church."

"Oh, right. You mean that time you were nosy?"

He smirks. "You two weren't doing a good job of hiding anything."

"No, I don't guess we were."

"What were you fighting about?"

"Babies," I reply.

He frowns.

"He'd just found out that I wasn't honest with him. I still feel bad about that."

Chapter Twenty-Four

Bexley
2019

I slide my black coat on, flipping the collar up to protect my neck from the chilling wind after we step out of the car. Snow crunches beneath my heels and icy air seeps down in my lungs.

"When are you and my grandson going to have one of those?" Ma asks, holding on to my arm as we walk past some kids while we head toward the church. We take her every Sunday, and every Sunday she asks me the same thing. Taking her also means we have to come to this side of town, which I hate because it brings up too many memories.

"Ma," Samuel says, looking at me sympathetically. I love Ma, but I wish she'd stop asking. Besides, we've only been trying for a year or so. Plus, it's not like we do it every single night. I pat her arm. "It'll happen when it happens, Ma," I say as we take the steps.

"It won't happen if you're not having sex," she blurts out as we walk through the doors. I take in a deep breath, trying to control my embarrassment. I look to the ceiling in prayer and hear the priest clear his throat as we move past him.

Patting Ma's hand, I remove her arm and let her walk in front of me down the pew. Paul, his wife, Ellen, and their three children are already here.

He kisses Ma's cheek when we near. I lean by them and kiss Ellen's in hello, waving to the littles, who aren't so little anymore. before greeting Paul with a cheek kiss also.

It's always a cheek kiss around here. It's just the way we all are. You see someone you love, you kiss their cheek when you say hello.

"Good to see you guys," Paul says.

"Likewise," Samuel returns. "How's everything?"

"Good," Paul replies. We take our seats as Ma rumbles through her purse for candy to give to the kids.

Samuel leans in my ear as we sit down. "We can try for those after this if you'd like?" he says, his deep voice sending chills down my spine. I smile, turning toward him, and then I catch the sight of someone sitting over on the other row. Samuel kisses my neck, oblivious to the devil occupying this Godly place.

It's been a while since I've laid eyes on him. In a black suit and tie he looks too good to be true. I know under that collar are tattoos, and behind those eyes was once a boy I was infatuated with.

Shit.

Insurgent

He doesn't turn his head, his chin is lifted, his face expressionless, but his sight is directly on me. I'm the first to look away, standing with everyone else as the service begins.

I slide my gloves back on as the service wraps up. The massive building is filled with the sounds of people talking amongst themselves, asking about Christmas plans and how their week was. We didn't leave our seats during the exchange of peace and neither did Danny.

"There's your brother," I say to Samuel as we stand up.

He looks at me. "You would notice him first." My heart drops.

"Excuse me?" I ask.

He doesn't reply, but I see his jaw ticking. His remark confuses me. I haven't shown any affection toward another man, only Samuel. Our marriage has been great, for the most part, over these past few years. I mean, we've had some rocky times, but always come out on top and together.

We get to the end of the row and I see Johnny also. Not sure who this other person is with them.

"Oh, Danny," Ma says with the sweetest smile on her lips. Pink looks good on her cheeks.

She loves all of her boys, but she's always had a special place in her heart for Danny.

"Ma." Danny gives her a gentle hug and she grabs his face, kissing each cheek.

"I just saw you last week," he says to her, like she's overreacting. I feel my brow furrow.

I don't know why I figured since we never see him, the rest of them didn't either. I wonder if Paul sees him often, too.

"Danny," Paul greets. Danny shakes his brother's hand and kisses Ellen on the cheek before ruffling the two boys' hair and scooping his niece up. She giggles, leaning into her uncle.

"Little brother," Danny nods at Samuel, "how are you?"

"Fine," Samuel says. "When did you get back in town?"

Huh?

Samuel knew he was out of town. Am I the only one who doesn't talk to Danny?

"Last week," Danny replies, his eyes landing on me. "Bexley, how's the shop?" And he shocks the living fuck out of me when he quickly reaches in, kissing the side of my face in greeting.

Something inside of me ignites.

A black flame.

Hidden feelings.

My whole nervous system.

The cheek kiss has never applied to us.

And I swear I hear a faint gasp from somewhere, but that's just my ears. No one would do that where Danny could hear them.

"Fine, Danny," I reply with my fists balled in my trench coat's pockets, acting as though he didn't just bring me back to life.

"Good. Let's go eat, yeah?" He looks at little Samantha and tickles her stomach, earning another giggle from her.

He walks in front with Samantha in his arms and his two "dogs" follow behind. Ma grabs Paul's arm and Ellen gets her other kids in line. Samuel and I are last to go.

"You've been talking with Danny?" I ask.

He nods. "Of course. He's my brother."

"You didn't tell me this."

"Why does it matter?"

"Because I assumed you didn't have a relationship."

"You assumed wrong," he says, his tone clipped.

I don't appreciate it. I touch his arm, moving us to the side. "Hey, what's the deal with you?" I ask lowly so no one else can hear us.

Samuel looks at me, and for the first time, I see it. Not think it, or wonder, but really see it.

He knows.

He lifts his chin. "Let's not pretend like your whole world doesn't light up when he's around, Bex."

Guilt swims heavy in my veins, but I try to keep it off my face. "I don't know what you're talking about, and I don't appreciate what you're insinuating. I've been nothing but committed to this marriage and honest with you."

He laughs before leaning near my ear. "Is that why you've been taking birth control?"

I swallow.

"So, I don't want to have a child right now. That has nothing to do with Danny."

People walk past us as the family waits outside. The cold wind has entered in through the doors, sending a chill down my neck.

Samuel tilts his head. "Why not just say that then?"

"Because I thought that's what you wanted." I lower my voice. "I didn't want to disappoint you."

"So, you lie to me? Trick me?" My husband is the softer side of the O'Brien boys, but right now, the way he's looking at me, it's far from easygoing.

"It was wrong, Samuel. I get that. I'm sorry."

He nods. "Yeah, well, at least you get it," he says sarcastically. "Makes me wonder what else you've been keeping from me. I'll meet you outside."

My heart sinks at his flat tone, his disgusted expression. I've never seen him look at me like that and it hurts, but I deserve it.

I watch him walk away, then I look down at the floor. I haven't been taking birth control this whole time. I did stop, but then something made me start taking it again. I narrow my eyes toward the floor.

Wait, he knew I was taking birth control?

Then why make that comment earlier that we can go home and make a kid? Why keep up the pretenses? Why wait until now to call me out?

"Trouble in paradise?" I hear behind me. I turn to look at Danny leaning against the pew, confusion obviously on my face. "Left these," he says, showing me his gloves. I see the skeleton tattoo covering the tops of his fingers and hand. He must have slipped past us. I didn't even notice.

"We're fine," I reply.

"Yeah," he says disbelievingly. He slides his hands into his pockets. We stare at each other for a moment. I feel like we do this every time we see each other, and it's been a while. Soaking up the things about one another that have changed. New wrinkles around the eyes, tattoos, longer hair.

My hair's in a tight ponytail, my lips covered in a shade of nude. He seems to study all of this about me, looking over my cream dress and black heels, while I look at the tie around his neck, the black shirt he wears, his dark hair, and even the watch he has on his wrist.

My eyes go back to his. There's so much there that we don't say. An entire life's worth of unspoken words.

I lift a brow, and without another sound, I turn and walk out of the church to my husband who without a doubt knows I'm in love with his brother.

Still.

Chapter Twenty-Five

Bones
One month three days missing

"Ma said that?" I ask her.

"Yep, right when we neared the priest."

I laugh. Damn, I miss her. I hope she's getting along okay right now. God, I swear if Trig hurts her.

"I was so embarrassed."

"Yeah, well…the man knows how kids are made."

"Still," she says.

"Why were you lying to him?" I ask, trying to mock indifference.

She shrugs. "We tried to have them at first, and then something in me changed. I just thought maybe it wasn't the right time. I wish I could take it back. I wish we would have had children. At least now I'd have a piece of Samuel. Now I have nothing but his memory."

Guilt is not a feeling I'm familiar with. I've taken lives, I've had lives taken with just one word, and I've never felt bad. I've never felt guilty. When you're in the type of business I am, you have to understand what comes with it.

None of the people I've killed would have died if they made better choices and that's all there is. But my brother was a good man. He wasn't like me; he deserved to live to an old age with his grandkids surrounding him and a woman who loved him equally by his side.

I have guilt for that.

I didn't kill my baby brother, but I am the reason he's gone.

So...there's that.

And don't think I meant that woman is Bexley, because it's not. She loved Samuel in her own way, but not the way she loves me, and I'll never be convinced otherwise.

She moves away from the window where we stand, and I feel colder. She's lost weight. Her waist is thinner, her face, too. I watch as she leans down and places another log in the stove. Amber twirls upward, a piece popping out and landing on the floor of the cabin. She turns sideways, crossing her arms.

She's as beautiful to me now as she was when she was seventeen. Better actually. She looks away from the fire, looking at me. My ankles are crossed, my back leans against the cool windowpane. She shivers, even though she's standing right by the fire.

I want to tell her to come here. I want to hold her. I long for her touch. So many years have flown by without it. Has she missed me as much as I have her? Has she dreamed about me? She licks her bottom lip and I push off the window, walking over to her. She doesn't move. I'm right in front of her now, and I start to lean in, and then her eyes close and she says, "Danny." Her face is pained. I nod, clear my throat, and walk over to the opposite window. I want to rip this whole goddamn place apart.

Chapter Twenty-Six

Bones
2019

The tension is thick between my brother and Bexley. I sensed it all through dinner, but everyone else seemed unaware. It's been a while since we've all sat at Ma's table and shared a meal. It's nice to have the kids running around. Ma's playing cards with Paul, and Ellen is cleaning the kitchen with Bexley. Sweep and Trig sit outside having a smoke and a beer.

"What's the deal with you two?" I ask Samuel, nodding my head toward the kitchen.

"Mind your business, Danny," he replies, deadpan.

"Hey, is that any way to talk to your big brother?" I say, placing my hand over my chest.

He scoffs and shakes his head as his eyes go to the table. "What are you doing with yourself these days?" he asks me, his voice laced with attitude.

"Running the bar," I reply, wondering where he's getting at. We still meet up on Wednesdays and Sundays, not sure why he's all of a sudden interested in what the fuck I do.

I know, I shouldn't have asked about him and Bexley. It is their business. I laugh to myself, remembering a time when Bexley said curiosity killed the cat. God, what a lifetime ago that was. Two kids throwing rocks at windows, having no idea just how connected we would eventually become.

So, I shouldn't have questioned them… Either way, he needs to watch his smart mouth.

His eyes jump back to mine. "Is that what you tell people?"

I narrow my eyes. "Watch it, Samuel. Don't go poking your nose in places you don't want to be poking."

"You think we all don't know?" he asks. "You think word hasn't gotten around Postings that you're up to no good? Look at you, Danny. You look like a fucking criminal."

I sit up, calmly linking my fingers together on the table, leaning closer to him as I tilt my head. "You think because I don't look like a pretty boy, Samuel, I'm a criminal? You think because I don't get up every morning, kiss my sweet little wife, and throw on slave clothes to go work for another man that I'm up to no good?

"You sit here with your fake blue-collar life and judge me? You wouldn't last a day in my world. Get the fuck out of my face, you disrespectful little prick."

He smirks. "Yeah, Danny. Who the fuck wants to live in your world?" He stands up, snatching his coat from the back of the chair. "Bex, come the hell on. We're leaving."

"Don't talk to her like that," I say in a low warning tone.

He looks at me with fire in his eyes. "I think you forget that she's *my* wife."

I sit back, rubbing the pad of my thumb and index finger together. "I'm very aware of that, brother. Still. Don't talk to her like that," I warn with the smallest shake of my head, my eyes blinking once.

"Fuck you, *brother*." He emphasizes the word *brother* and exits through the dining room door. I ball my fists, trying to remember he's my blood.

I can't hurt him.

I turn to look behind me, seeing Bexley appear at the doorway leading into the kitchen with a towel in her hand.

My eyes jump down the length of her body before I turn back. "Does he always speak to you like that?"

"What did you do?" she asks accusingly.

"Don't start this shit with me, Bex."

She barges into the room, tossing the towel at my chest before she grabs her coat from the other chair.

"Why the hell did you come today?" she asks, anger slipping in her tone. "To fuck with me?" She twirls the long coat, sliding her arms into the sleeves.

Black's definitely her color.

"Listen, love, it's not my fault your little world isn't as perfect as you make it out to be. Crystal is pretty, but it shatters," I say. I loosen my tie. "Don't get cut." I wink and cluck my tongue as she lifts her chin at me.

"My little world was just fine without you in it. And don't ever call me love again."

I stand up, the chair moving when the backs of my legs hit it. I stalk toward her. Her feet carry her toward the wall. My hand goes above her head and I look down at her pretty pissed off face.

I would kiss her if she wasn't my brother's wife. God, I would do more than that. My fingers burn with the need to dig into her flesh, bend her over, and press against her.

My eyes go to her lips.

Hers go to mine.

I haven't been this intimate with her in years. Her face is so close, I can feel her breath slipping over my skin. My pulse pounds to a steady beat and my hand twitches to wrap around her throat, applying just enough pressure while I kiss her smart mouth.

"Have you ever told him?" I ask. "Our little secret? Does my brother know that you knew I burnt a man alive, and yet you still gave me everything?"

The kids run by the door, and before I can blink, she shoves me back with force.

Her chest heaves, and her mouth hangs open slightly. I stand still as I watch her. She looks toward the door before looking back at me. "You're a fool, Danny."

"Am I the fool, though?" I ask cynically. "Who's the one married to the wrong person?"

She slaps me. My whole face stings, and I love it. I move my jaw and look back at her, and it's her expression that makes me snap out of it.

I don't know what the fuck I'm thinking. I know I'm no saint, but she's my brother's wife. I have some morals.

"You son of a bitch," she seethes. "Why do you keep doing this? Huh? Is it fun to you? Hurting people?" She shakes her head, looking at me as though I'm lower than tits on a snake. "You make me sick."

"Get the fuck out of here, Bexley, before I do something I regret." She has no idea how being this close to her makes me feel.

"Oh, now who's talking to me disrespectfully? Leave us alone, Danny. Leave *us* alone before you fuck up everything I've worked for." And then like we weren't just inches apart, as if we both didn't almost die to touch the other only moments ago, she walks out without a second glance back.

Chapter Twenty-Seven

Bones
2019

Monday is business as usual. We sit at the round table, the money counter a steady noise. Bags of money sit near the wall that's already been counted and bound. I hit the joint, sitting back in my chair with my shirt sleeves rucked. I watch as Trig and Sweep stack hundreds, Trig telling us about a time he put a bunch of firecrackers in David's, his foster parent's, trunk. David's nothing more than fertilizer now.

"Scared the piss out of him. He ran off the road and hit the damn power pole. We were out of power for half the day, but it was worth it," he says.

Sweep nods with a slight smirk. "I remember that. Didn't know it was you, though."

"Of course not. I never get caught."

I reach up, putting the joint in the ashtray as Moretti walks out of his office. "Better get to the bank with all that before they close," he says.

I lift my chin. "Where you headed?"

He looks at me. "Don't worry about it. Get to the bank."

I feel my eye twitch. "Yeah, okay."

He looks at Nugget. "You're coming with me," he says.

Nugget smiles, like he just won over daddy. I wink at him because I love fucking with that man. His smile falls, and he points at me behind Moretti's back.

I smirk, watching them as they leave.

"Looks like somebody's got a new favorite," Trig says teasingly.

I keep my eyes on the door they just walked out of, wondering where they're headed. Moretti's changed over the last few years. He's sloppy, and the fact he's picking Nugget to go on these little secret business meetings instead of me has me curious.

"You never tell us any stories about your childhood," Trig says.

"The hell you wanna know about my childhood for?"

He shrugs. "Why not?" He slides a paper band around the stack of bills he just grabbed from the machine. He's right. I never talk about my childhood. There are things even Sweep doesn't know.

There're just certain things a person keeps to themselves. We all have secrets, and I don't think that's a bad thing. But I also don't think opening up a little could hurt anyone. Trig's always telling me his psychiatrist says it's good to let things out.

I nod, tilting my head in a shrug. "I was raised in the Catholic church. Had a bunch of people in and out of the house a lot. My dad was a bookie for Moretti when Moretti was deep into the gambling world, until he got murdered, that is."

"You never told me about that," Sweep says.

"Yeah, well, I'm telling you now." I grab my smoke from the ashtray. "I loved the man. Wanted to be just like him. I'd lie on the floor playing with Matchbox cars while he worked. He'd tell me all kinds of stories about Ireland and what his life was like over there. I soaked up everything that man said, like his words were bible." I look down at the table for a moment, recalling a time he had some men over for dinner. I tell Sweep and Trig about it, wearing a smile. "I wasn't supposed to be listening, but you know me by now. I'm not one to follow rules.

"Laughing and dirty talk went around the table as they all ate, licking their fingers and drinking their whiskey. One man was talking shit about another who apparently wasn't there, and my dad turned and looked at him, pointed, and said, 'What you're saying about Miller says a whole lot more about you than it does Miller.'

"Everyone stopped talking and Moretti looked at the guy who was running his mouth and told him to shut the hell up. He said, 'You don't talk about a man who isn't here to defend himself.' I knew right then, Moretti, like me, had respect for my dad. Hence, why he got revenge for his death."

"How so?" Trig asks.

I look over at him. "He had them murdered. Them and their families."

"How'd he find out who did it? Killed your parents, I mean," Sweep says.

"Me. The men were stupid and didn't have on a mask, so I knew exactly what they looked like." I pass the joint to him. "I remembered the one man had a black diamond ring on his finger.

"A week later, I was walking out of Ma's house and saw a note left on the doorstep, along with an old teddy bear. The thing had shoes on and a black t-shirt," I recall. "Note read, 'A present for you.'" I wave my hand in the air. "I noticed a slit in the back of the bear, and stuffed inside was a bloody finger with a black diamond ring on it. I tossed the finger, kept the ring." I hold my hand up, showing the ring. I've been wearing it a lot lately. It reminds me to keep my shit together. A time will come for change, but now is not that time. "I never said anything about it to my brothers or Ma."

"Or me," Sweep says, offering the joint to Trig, but he declines.

"Or you," I say.

"I knew in a sense of what it meant, but when I ran into Moretti on the street one day, he confirmed it. The finger was the gift, a show of respect." I feel my eyes slant as I stare toward the door. "But that was a long time ago. Moretti's changed."

"Yeah, I've noticed," Sweep says.

I look over at Trig when I hear the pop of his rubber band.

"What the hell's wrong with you?"

He shakes his head, his eyes looking down at my hand. I crack my knuckles and stand up. "You two get this shit to the bank. I'm going to take a ride."

Chapter Twenty-Eight

Bexley
One month three days missing

Talking to Danny like this seems like a daydream trapped inside of a nightmare. We didn't speak a whole lot when we were first taken, because I had too much hate and hurt inside of me. He wanted to kiss me just now. He almost tried and I couldn't do it. I can't pretend like everything is okay. Samuel died.

You know you wanted him to, though.

Looking back on our life together has been a therapy session I didn't know I needed until now. I feel lighter for it, and I hope he does, too.

I lied to Danny, though, when I told him it just didn't feel like the right time to have a baby with Samuel. It's something that I couldn't admit before, but now that Samuel's gone and my life has changed and might end soon, I can let the truth come out.

I've always wanted Danny's babies, even when I knew that wasn't possible. I've prayed about it. I've asked God to forgive me more times than I care to admit for my feelings for Danny. What a life, huh? Married to one brother while longing for the other.

And he knew.

Samuel knew.

Danny stands by the window, his shoulders tense. "I'm sorry," I say.

He turns to look at me. "I want to kiss you. I want to feel you. I can't fucking stand being alone with you and not touching you."

I swallow.

"And I'm *not* sorry," he says.

Chapter Twenty-Nine

Bexley
2019
(Sunday)

I shut the truck door and Samuel holds the gate open for me after he walks through. We didn't talk on the way home. We're about to fight, and after what happened with Danny, I've got the energy. I can't believe he said that to me.

"Have you ever told him?" he asks. *"Our little secret? Does my brother know that you knew I burnt a man alive, and yet you still gave me everything?"*

God, he has no idea how angry he makes me. What would Samuel think of me if he knew that I knew how evil Danny could be, and yet I still chose to be with him? I don't know if he'd understand. I mean, he knows I'm not clueless about what Danny does, but he has no idea how far back his brother's sins go.

Samuel unlocks the door, and as soon as we both step inside, I turn to him.

"You know I married you, right?" I say to him, crossing my arms over my chest. "I picked you, would still pick you any day, but don't you ever talk to me like I'm your little dog in front of your family again."

"You mean in front of Danny?" he questions.

"I mean in front of any of them. What is this obsession with you thinking there's something going on between your brother and me?" My voice is calm. "I would never do anything to hurt you. You know that."

He looks to the floor and exhales. "I know. I just wonder sometimes if I make you happy enough. You're different when he's around. Your demeanor changes instantly like you're hyperaware of him." He looks back at me. "I'm envious of the way you look at him."

Crystal is pretty, but it shatters.

And that's exactly what my heart does.

My knees grow weak, my soul cries.

What have I done?

I feel the shake in my fingers, the ache in my chest.

Sure, Danny and I have chemistry and a history that we can't change, but what Samuel and I've built together is special and engraved in time. I would never want to hurt this love.

Intentionally.

It's sweet and warm.

"Samuel, do you not see the way I look at you?" I slowly slide my coat off my shoulders. "The day I said yes to marrying you, I was all in from that very moment." I step out of my shoes. "You're my husband, the man I chose to live my life with." I reach behind me and unzip my dress. "Nothing else matters." I slide the cream cloth down, slipping it over my hips and stepping out of it. "I love you."

Samuel looks at my body as I unclasp my bra, letting it tickle down my arms on the way off. "Make love to me."

He reaches out and pulls me to him so my breasts press against his dress shirt. "I'm sorry I talked to you like that."

"You're forgiven," I reply with a small smile.

"Good," he says, kissing my lips before he scoops me up and heads to the stairs. For the night, I forget about the man who lives in the darkest part of my soul.

The warm sun shines in through the window, burning bright against my face. My eyes flutter open and I blink. I stretch my arms, feeling the empty space beside me. Samuel's already off to work. I roll over, sighing and gripping the pillow as I think about yesterday.

I open my hand, looking over my palm. It felt good to slap Danny like that. It also hurt not to say I was sorry.

Regardless, I think he liked it. God, I hate myself. I hate everything about this.

Why can't he go away and never come back? Why does he keep slipping into my life?

Because you're married to his brother, dummy. You're his family.

I groan into the pillow as my phone rings. Reaching over, I blow my hair from my face and grab it, blinking and stretching my eyes to try to see the name. It's my uncle. He calls once a week, and I visit him a few times a month. The man who took me in after my mom died gave me a good life. I love him for trying to raise a kid who was heartbroken and having a hard time finding her place in the world. Especially when he was only in his twenties at the time.

"Hello," I say, sounding groggy from sleep, stress, and needing a drink even though it's seven a.m.

"Did I wake you?" he asks.

"No, I was just lying here. How are you?"

"I'm fine, sweetheart. How are things with you?"

I contemplate telling him how things really are, but then I decide against it. Hale has never liked Danny. He won't be happy to know he's causing trouble between Samuel and me.

So I go the easy way.

"I'm doing well." I throw the covers off and head into the bathroom. "How's the family?" I ask.

Insurgent

After the conversation with my Uncle Hale about his kids and now wife, Trinity, work, and Samuel, I take a shower and slip on a black jumpsuit with cream heels. I blow-dry my thick hair and do a messy side braid, applying some light makeup before heading down to the kitchen. A note sits on the counter from Samuel.

Sorry about yesterday. Not about last night.
-Love S.

I smile, grabbing my tan coat and sliding it on. I slip my phone into my pocket, feeling a piece of paper when I do. The paper feels soft against my skin as I remove my hand. My heart deflates to the pit of my stomach.

It's the one from Danny telling me to meet him in the alley all those years ago. The words are faded now, because it's been to the dry cleaners a few times. How it survived, I don't know.

I exhale, walk over to the stove, and switch it on. Pressing the paper against the eye, I watch it ignite before walking over to the sink. I drop it in, staring at it as it burns, and I find myself wishing that the way I feel about him would burn along with it.

Paige P. Horne

Coffee in hand, I step into the shop. I place my coffee and keys onto the counter and remove my coat, hanging it on the coat rack. Firing up my Mac, I slide the stool over and search through my work emails as the heater kicks on, sending a cozy warmth throughout the shop. I have several order requests and some junk mail to delete and I need to talk with Billie.

I start on the order requests first, and before I know it, I'm immersed in my work. A lot of our clients are rich assholes from the city who fuck their secretary but make sure to do something nice for their wife once a week just so the wife knows how special she is.

It's a shitty reality, but it is reality.

My day moves along quickly. Billie comes by with eggs from her chickens and brings me fresh garlic and herbs from her greenhouse.

"I know if there's ever an apocalypse I'm coming to your house."

She laughs. "You need to come out and have a glass of wine with me. Mike bought me some cows last week and we've got five pigs now."

"Good lord," I say. "I'll take you up on that. Samuel will love to see it."

After Billie leaves, I have a few walk-ins. Some chefs of the local restaurants in town and some customers I see once a week who want to replenish their own flowers throughout their home.

The afternoon flies and I realize I haven't spoken to Samuel about supper. I think I'll cook us some spaghetti with the fresh herbs Billie brought. I grab my phone, finding his name and hitting the call button. My eyes go to the six beautifully arranged bouquets I put together, ready for delivery as the phone rings. It's his voicemail.

"Hey, honey. I wanted to see if you'd like spaghetti for supper. Call me back. Love you." I put my phone down and grab my watering can before I go around the shop hydrating the plants when Don, our delivery driver, walks in.

"Good evening," he says. "These ready to go?"

"Hey, Don. Yes. Those are for Mrs. Blanton on Cotton Avenue."

"Great. I'll get them over to her." Mrs. Blanton loves fresh flowers in her home. There isn't a room you'll go in without seeing a vase or two.

"See you tomorrow," I tell him, knowing that's his last delivery for the day. He gives me a wave as he walks out with the crate of flowers. The shop phone starts to ring. I hop down from the stepladder and walk to the desk.

"A-Street Flowers," I answer, holding the phone between my cheek and shoulder as I write a reminder to order some more vases and ribbons.

"Hello?" I say again, dropping the pen.

I narrow my eyes when I hear heavy breathing on the other end. Chills run down my arms, and my spine straightens when I get the odd sense of someone watching me. I turn to look out the window but see no one there.

"Hello?" I repeat.

The phone goes dead and I drop it from my shoulder, catching it with my hand. I narrow my eyes as I gaze out of the windows, and then I walk over to the door and lock it, putting the closed sign up quickly.

I'm probably just overreacting. It's probably just some kids prank calling.

Do kids do that anymore?

I shake my head and take a breath, walking over to grab my phone when someone bangs on the door behind me. I nearly jump out of my skin as I turn around. I sigh in relief when I see it's my husband. Slipping my phone into my pocket, I walk over to the door to let Samuel in.

"Jesus, you scared me." I laugh as I place my hand on the lock.

He smiles. "Obviously. You closed up already?"

"Well, someone called and…" I look behind Samuel when a car rides by and my eyes grow wide when I see a masked man stick out a machine gun. Bullets ring through the windows, shattering glass. "Samuel!" I scream, ducking.

"Get down!" he yells, covering his head, but there's nothing to protect him, nothing to shield him from the firing bullets as they destroy the shop. I quickly crawl over to my desk, bowing my own head as I slide over broken glass to get behind it. I cover my mouth in horror as Samuel's body jerks from the bullets hitting him. Potted plants burst, and soil flies into the air, showering my husband and me.

My eyes blur, and my hands shake as something is tossed into the shop before the car speeds off. The bullets stop, glass still rains down, and hanging plants swing in the air. I jump up. "Samuel," I say, running over to him. There's so much blood.

Too much blood.

"Hey," I say. He looks at me, his eyes wide.

"Bex, I don't want to die," he says, his chest heaving.

"You're not going to." I grab my phone from my pocket, quickly dialing 911, rambling off my address and what happened. "Hurry. Please, hurry," I beg, hanging up. I sniff, rubbing my nose before I stand and grab some towels from under the counter. Glass crunches beneath my feet as I hear sirens in the distance. "They're coming," I say, applying pressure to some of the gunshots.

Blood comes out of his mouth. "Bex," he says.

"Samuel." I start to cry. "You're going to be okay."

He grips onto my hand. "I love you," I say. "I love you so much. You mean so much to me. Our life together has been all I could have asked for. It's always been you, Samuel." I stare into his eyes, wanting him to know that I mean what I say. I become the best fucking actress of all time, just so he doesn't leave this earth thinking anything other than what I'm telling him.

He looks at me as I squeeze his hand. His eyes dance over my face, and then like a light losing its glow, my husband's life vanishes before me as his head slouches and his eyes lose focus.

"No, no, no, no." I bow my head, resting it against his. "Don't leave me." I wrap my arms around him, sobbing uncontrollably. My whole body quakes, my soul bleeding as I kiss his face and hands. I see the lights from the ambulance reflect off the walls of the shop and people run in here.

"Miss?" a man says to me.

I look up. "It's missus," I reply. I look back down at my best friend. The one who did everything he could to try to make me happy. "He's gone. Oh God. He left…" My hands shake, covered in his blood. My ears ring, and my mind races.

"Ma'am, let us take care of this."

"Take care of what?" I ask. "There's nothing to take care of."

"What's your name?" A woman appears with kind eyes. Eyes like Samuel's.

Insurgent

He's so kind, so caring.

"Bexley O'Brien. This is my husband."

My husband.

My sweet, handsome husband.

What happened?

"Mrs. O'Brien, are you hurt?"

I look down at my body, seeing his blood on my chest and arms. "I don't think so."

She gives me a small smile. "Good," she says. "I understand this is difficult, but we need to get Mr. O'Brien out of here."

I nod, looking down at him again. Memories of our life together flood my mind. We had it all. The friendship. The love. The loyalty. We laughed a lot. Life was easy with him, and now it's over. He's too young. We're too young.

I kiss his cheek and forehead, moving back as someone comes in with a stretcher. I feel the glass cutting into my skin, but I don't care. I don't care about anything.

My eyes go under the table and I see the bottle that was tossed in here. Tears river down my face in thick heartbreak. I stare at the floor they just lifted Samuel from.

My mind spaces, going as blank as a fresh sheet of paper. My heart freezes over. I don't want to live in a world where he doesn't. He was the one good thing. He was the good.

Blackness washes over my soul.

Who did this?

Why?

Did Samuel know I loved him?

Did he understand that he made my life better?

We'd just made up; we'd just had a great night. How quickly life changes. How unimportant everything seems. This shop, these fucking flowers. This stupid outfit, these shoes.

I kick them off as someone talks to me. I look at their face, but I don't hear what they're saying. I don't want to talk to them.

"Give her some space." A raspy voice comes through the ringing in my ears and I look up and see a blurry Danny. I don't want him. I want Samuel. He bends down, but I push away.

"You will let me carry you out of here. Don't fight me."

How is he here?

Why is he here?

I sob uncontrollably, giving in.

"It's okay," he says, lifting me into his arms like I'm a small child.

"He's gone, Danny. They took him from me."

"What the fuck happened?" I hear Paul and I turn my head.

"Bex," he says, his face showing heartbreak. I can't do anything but cry. My body trembles painfully. He jabs his eyes with his fingers as he looks at the battered shop, holding his hand over his mouth.

I hurt. God, I hurt. Please wake me from this nightmare.

Please, God, if you bring him back, I swear I'll do anything. I'll do anything.

"We need to ask her some questions," a cop says.

"Not fucking now, you don't," Danny says, walking us out of the door.

Johnny jumps out of the car and quickly walks around to open the door.

"I can get in myself," I say.

"I know," Danny replies but ignores me when he bends, placing me inside. I look down at my bloody hands as Johnny gets in the driver's side and Danny shuts the door. Blood dries in between lines, sticking in between my fingers, covering my wedding band.

"His ring," I say as the ambulance starts to drive off.

"What?" Johnny asks, looking back at me.

"His ring, Johnny. I need his ring." I hurry to open the door.

"Bex," he says. I step out, barefoot, seeing Danny and Paul look my way in my peripheral as I push away from the door, running toward the ambulance. I only get to the end of the car before I feel arms wrap around me.

"His ring," I say. "I want his ring." I try to pull the hands away from me, digging into skin.

"Bexley, we'll get it," Danny says to me.

I claw at his hands. "I don't want them to lose it," I say, trying to get out of his hold.

He squeezes tighter, and I break more, my knees giving out, hitting the hard pavement.

"They won't lose it," he says. "I promise."

My lungs ache, my heart in too much pain I can hardly breathe. I'm useless.

I grip at the clothing covering my heart, wishing this pain would stop. "I can't breathe." I say, placing a hand on the ground.

"It's okay. You're going to be okay," Danny says.

I shake my head. "That's exactly what I told him," I cry. "I lied to him, Danny."

I don't say what I lied to him about. I don't admit that I told Samuel it was always him, when truthfully, it's always been the man holding me right now.

And I hate him, but I hate me more. I put my face in my hands as a painful sob rolls from my throat, and then sickness rises, and I puke.

Acid burns my throat, and I spit, wiping my mouth with my hand.

No one says anything at first, and then Paul says, "Jesus, get her up."

I'm lifted again, unable to fight anymore. Once in the car, I look out at the shop with its broken windows.

"Here," Johnny says, handing me a towel. I grab it, wiping my face and blowing my nose. Cops move in and out, yellow tape is hung, and Paul speaks with some detective. All the while, a bottle rests under a table with a note in it, and I pray they don't find it because I need to know what it says. I need to know who did this and what kind of message they were sending.

Were those bullets meant for me? Was I supposed to die instead of Samuel? Tears fall down my face, and I bow my head.

"You know Bones will find out who did this, Bexley. This won't go unpunished."

I sit up. "Bones?" I ask. "You mean Danny?"

He doesn't answer me as Danny opens the car door and gets in, looking over at me. "Get us out of here, Sweep."

Sweep?

Bones?

What are these names?

"The fuck is Trig?" Danny says as Sweep hauls ass away from the crime scene.

Oh, God. Crime scene.

"I don't know. He left the bar earlier. Maybe he's at the warehouse."

I look out the window as heartache slides down my face.

"Call him and see," Danny says.

The sun has gone away.

The sky is a blue black as it transitions from day to night, just as my world transitions from life to death. Johnny speaks. "He's at the warehouse."

Danny doesn't respond to Johnny. Instead, he talks to me. "I'm going to let you be for the moment. But soon, you will talk to me. For now, we'll go get his ring."

Chapter Thirty

Bexley
2019

I climb into the shower, holding my hands out as the scalding water washes away my husband's blood. It rains down, coloring the water in crimson heartache. I run my hands down my face, my tears chapping my skin. Life will never be the same for me. I grab the locket necklace I have around my neck, running my fingers over his ring that now resides there.

After my freak-out, Johnny drove us to the hospital and I was able to get Samuel's wedding band before I insisted they take me home.

Not without a fight.

"You're not going to your fucking house, Bexley."

"You're not going to tell me what to, Danny."

He exhales. "It's dangerous. We don't know the situation yet."

"I want to be close to my husband."

"Your husband's not there, Bexley."

I reach back and slap him with everything inside of me as we stand in the garage. It echoes off the cement walls.

"Did you have something to do with this?" I ask.

"What?" he says, stepping closer to me. "You watch your next words, love."

"Johnny, take me home or I'll call a fucking cab."

"You're being unreasonable here. I'm just trying to protect you."

"Protect me?" I ask incredulously. "I think you're the reason I'm in this situation. I'm in more danger around you than I would be alone. How were you there so quickly, huh? How did you get there as soon as it happened? Were you watching me? Lurking around like some stalker?"

He doesn't say anything, and that answers my question. He had to have been there to see it. I need to get away from this mess.

"Johnny, you taking me home or what?"

Johnny looks at Danny. "Good God, can you make a decision by yourself, or does your whole life go by what this man tells you?"

Danny shakes his head. "Come on, Sweep. Let's take this stubborn ass home."

They checked the whole house out before I could even go inside. Danny had grabbed my coat and shoes from the shop, but I didn't care if I was cold or not. I deserve nothing but coldness in my life now. I had the best man a woman could want, and I didn't appreciate it enough.

Insurgent

And now he's gone.

Nothing but a memory for me. One that I will cherish forever. I lost two very important people in my life. My husband and my mother.

"Dear God."

Who am I supposed to talk to?

I lower myself into the tub, my body unable to hold me up. My knees hit the floor, and I fall forward, bowing my head as I tremble. "I just want you back," I cry. I look down at the floor, and then I remember.

The bottle.

My first thought as I put a beanie over my wet head is how will I sneak out without Danny's men seeing me. He's got people watching over the house, but they'll just have to follow me. Which won't be a bad thing considering there's someone apparently trying to kill me.

I put my long coat on over a t-shirt and jeans before sliding on a pair of slip-on Tracers. I grab my keys and head out the door. The frosty wind slices me in two as I walk to the SUV. Quickly climbing inside, I fire it up and speed away from the curb. Two cars follow me, and I'm sure they've told Danny I've left the house.

I hope the cops didn't find that bottle. I desperately want to know what the paper inside says. The more I think about it, the more I know this has Danny written all over it. Who knows who that man has pissed off over the years. Who knows what he's done.

I bite my lip. *I need to call Sam...*

"Jesus." I cover my mouth as my eyes tear up. Reality hits me like a ton of bricks. My husband's gone, and for a split moment I forgot. I wipe the tears from my face, hurt crushing my heart with a vise grip.

"I can't breathe." I press the gas harder, my eyes blur, and my mind blanks. My body reacts the way my soul wants, and cars blow the horn at me, shaking me out of it.

"Shit," I curse, realizing I'm running through a red light when a car slams on the brakes nearly sideswiping me. I pull over on the side of the road, yanking the car in park and getting out.

My breaths come in thick heaves, my body sweating even though it's cold out here. I cry and hold my chest. "I can't..."

I weep harder, holding on to the open door.

"Bexley!"

I hear someone, but my ears ring loud, my lungs ache, and my heart shrinks by the minute.

Hands touch my body. "You trying to leave me, too?"

I turn around and see Danny. "Come on, get in the car. I'll drive you home."

I shake my head. "I can't go home. I can't be there alone," I say, panic hitting me again.

I can't do it.

He looks over my face before he nods. "Okay. Come to my place then."

"No," I say, shaking my head. "I can't do that either."

"Well, what the fuck do you want to do, Bex?" he asks, throwing up his arms in defeat. "You don't want to go with me, and you don't want to go home. So tell me! What do you want?"

"Just leave me alone," I say, wiping a hand under my nose. I go to climb back into my car.

"No fucking way," he says, holding on to the door. "Get out. I'm driving you."

"I don't need you to drive me. I don't need anything from you. I need my husband. I need Samuel."

Danny flinches, like I've hit him, but I don't care. I've never wanted him less than I do right now. I need my life back. I need to wake the hell up from this god-awful nightmare.

His hard features show hurt, but then he says, "I know. But he was my brother, Bex, and I'm not standing by and letting his wife put herself in danger. He wouldn't want you hurt."

My chest caves and my eyes cast downward. "I'm the worst kind of hurt."

He grabs my hand and squeezes it, and I feel bad for being mean to the only person who's here for me. "I'm sorry," I say, my voice weak.

"You have nothing to be sorry for, love."

I look up at him and sniff. "How did this happen? How am I supposed to live without him, Danny?"

I cry more, even though I don't want to, and Danny says, "You wake up every day and you live. That's all you can do."

I shut my eyes, and I talk to the devil.

Have my soul, just give me my husband back.

The drive to Danny's bar is quiet. I could stay with Ma, but that house is like a tomb filled with memories. I can't handle that. I should stay with my uncle, who I talked to before I got a shower earlier, but he's got young kids now and a family and I don't want to intrude on any of them.

He assures me I wouldn't, but I know that's not true. The kids would want me to be chipper, and there's no way in hell I can act like I'm happy right now.

So, after a trip back to my house to grab some clothes, I'm heading to Danny's bar. We pull up to the curb and both of us climb out. I walk inside, noticing no one in here.

"Where are your customers?" I ask.

"I told Mae to close up for the night."

"I hope you didn't do that on my account."

"No. My brother just died, Bexley. I need to grieve just like you do."

God. I rub my forehead. "I'm an idiot. I'm sorry."

He doesn't respond as he places my bag on a table. "Want a drink?" he asks, walking around the bar.

"I don't think I can stomach it. If it's all the same to you, I'd rather go on up."

He nods. "Go right ahead."

I don't reply as I grab my bag and head up the stairs. Opening the door to his apartment, I walk in and narrow my eyes at the space. It's a loft. There's only one bed. Black curtains hang on the window, and the comforter matches. There's a dresser with a wooden box on top and a bedside table with a lighter and a lamp.

"Mae changed the sheets," I hear behind me.

"Where will you sleep?" I ask, removing my beanie and running a hand through my damp hair.

He nods toward his couch. I lift a brow, dropping my bag and turning to him. "I'm putting you out."

"No one puts me out."

"You're sleeping on your couch instead of your bed because of me, Danny."

He exhales, taking a sip of his drink. "I'm not going to sleep tonight anyway."

"I should go back home. This is stupid." I shake my head. "I'm a grown woman, for fuck's sake. I have a house." I lift my bag.

"If you leave, it's because you want to. You hear me?" he says.

I look at him and blink. He watches me, and then he walks over to his closet and grabs a throw and an extra pillow, tossing them onto the couch. He ignores me with his back faced my way and places his drink down and removes his shirt.

God, so different from the boy I used to be with. Back muscles and tattoos and even a few scars. I look away, trying to erase the tattoos and all the skin I just saw from my mind.

I feel so stupid right now, but it's too cold and too late to drive all the way to the north side of town, so I take my bag into the bathroom and I shut the door. I remove my coat before sliding my jeans and t-shirt off. Unzipping my bag, I grab one of Samuel's t-shirts and bring it to my face, breathing in deeply. It smells like grass and laundry detergent. My eyes water and I sit on the edge of the tub, thinking about his face, his eyes, the way his lips curved when he smiled. I wipe my cheek and slide the shirt over my head. I grab a pair of black night pants out of my bag.

Opening the door, I walk out, seeing Danny has turned the lights off except for a small lamp. He lies on the couch, facing away from me with a small fan circulating the room. I walk over to the bed and pull the covers back, climbing inside and noticing the sheets smell like fresh Downy. This brings me the slightest bit of comfort.

I curl into the fetal position and stare at the glowing lamp across the room. Pain simmers in my chest like a boiling pot and I let tears fall because I simply can't stop them.

Chapter Thirty-One

Trig

I step into my house, sweat rolling down my spine, my hands shaking.

"Where the fuck are you?" I call out.

"Back here," he says. The house is dark. I walk toward the hall, hitting the table beside the couch and knocking over some beer bottles. I leave them and walk to the kitchen. He stands in a black mask holding on to an AK-47. The back door is still open.

"Why did you come here?" I ask. "What were you thinking?" I walk over and pull the door closed.

"I was thinking I needed to get rid of this damn gun."

"So, you come here?"

"Look, I did you a favor. Don't fucking stand there and act like I work for you now."

I shake my head, grabbing the sides of it as I pace back and forth. "Did anyone see you? Was he there?"

"The girl did, and I'm not sure. I didn't see his car."

"Did you kill her? Is she dead?"

He grabs the mask and pulls it off. "I was going too fast, I don't know."

"You don't know? How the fuck don't you know?"

"I was driving and shooting the fucking gun. I let off a whole clip on the place. It had to hit her."

I wipe the sweat from my brow. "If he finds out who we are before I'm able to get him, then we're dead, you know that, right? We're fucking dead!" I hit the cabinet, punching a hole through the thing.

I've got to hurry. "You're going to help me get him."

"No, the hell I'm not. I did my part. I took care of the girl and I tossed the bottle inside."

"Well, you don't know if she's dead. And the note is only going to fuel him. So, we've got to be quick with this. He'll be on a killing spree when he finds out she's dead. If she's dead. So I need your help in capturing him."

"Where the hell are you going to keep him? Here?"

"No, I've got a place. I just need you to help me get him there, and then you don't have to worry about anything else."

"Fine," he says. "I'll help you."

Chapter Thirty-Two

Bexley
One month three days missing

I stare at Danny as he stands across the room.

"Did you hear me?" he says.

"I hear you," I reply. I turn away because I just can't look at him. Doesn't he realize what he's asking of me? I'm a married—— am I married? My husband is gone. How does that work? I feel my ring on my finger and then I feel him. Standing behind me. When did he get so close? I start to shake. I start to think about everything at once and then his hand touches my neck. His words flow through my mind.

"I want to kiss you. I want to feel you. I can't fucking stand being alone with you and not touching you."

Goosebumps form on my arms and down my back as he moves hair away from my neck. His breath slides over my skin, like fog rolling over a grassy hill, and I hear him inhale. Want is powerful. Lust makes things blurry. Love is messy. His lips touch my neck and my eyes close. My breathing accelerates. My heart pounds like a drum. "After all this time, you still smell the same," he says. His voice, raspy, deep, sad. Like he's missed out on something. It sends a chill down my spine, awakening nerve endings that only he can. God, I've missed him so much. I can't possibly smell great right now, but I'm not going to argue about it. I feel his hand on my hip.

When you're accustomed to someone you love touching you, you don't really think about it. It's natural, like scratching an itch. But Danny has not touched me in so long. I have not felt this love in what feels like a lifetime. That simple feel of his hand on my hip is so noticed. My senses are hyperaware.

We're in a temporary madness. One that we both feel. One that we have felt before. We're like a volcano; we erupt and then subside. We have roots planted so deep that the strongest wind couldn't lift what we share. Our love is redamancy. We both love one another just as much as the other. It's returned in full. I can feel it pouring off of him.

He kisses along the back of my nape, lightly as if I'm cracked glass that could shatter and cut him at any moment.

And then I make a mistake.

I close my eyes.

And I see Samuel. I step away from Danny.

It hurts. I'm still raw.

What am I doing?

Have I lost my goddamn mind?

I'll never see him again, he'll never hold my hand, and I'll never feel the rough calluses on his palm or hear his keys drop on the counter before the thump of his boots hit the floor. He'll never come up behind me while I'm washing dishes. I'll never smell his scent—outdoors and a mixture of sweat.

He'd smell like fresh cut lumber sometimes. I loved that. He knew I loved a bowl of cereal just before bed. He knew my favorite candle scent and how I hated dirt on the bottom of my feet. He bought me bedroom shoes all the time. Fuzzy ones, ones that were like flip-flops. Ones that covered my whole feet up past my ankle. I have so many. I'll have to buy my own now.

The thought bothers me. It's stupid. I can buy my own bedroom shoes. I have before, but the ones he bought were… They meant more.

I can't disrespect him by giving in to my want for Danny. I can't do that.

"It's been a month."

Danny

"What?" I say. She looks back at me, a baffled hurt expression on her face. "We've been here a

month. Samuel has been dead for only a month."
She looks like she's about to freak out.

Oh.

"Yeah," I reply, getting the picture. She's not over him. Why would she be? She chose him over me. She decided to live her life with him. It pisses me off.

"One month, a few days," I say, licking my lips so I can taste her skin that I just kissed.

"I'm sorry," she says, her eyes filling with tears. She reaches out and touches my chest, looking at her hands placed there. "You don't know how torn I am." Her eyes go to mine. "I've loved you my whole life, Danny. But I married Samuel and now he's dead and I don't know what I feel about anything, but I know I loved him. I know that."

Why does she have to keep reminding me?

Doesn't she know that I hurt, too. That that kills me. That I've been suffering for years because she married my brother and not me.

"I know. I love you, too, but I can't do anything about loving you right now. I can't—"

I reach up and hold her hands against my chest. "I'd say I understood, but I don't. I've only ever loved you."

She swallows and a tear rolls down her cheek. I want to wipe it away, but I like holding her hands even though my wrists burn, my back hurts, and my head throbs.

"I don't know what to say to that," she says.

"There's nothing to say, love."

She blinks, nods, and drops her hands.

And I feel so sad in this moment. Like I've lost something so important and I have no idea how to get it back. I feel like Tom Hanks when he lost Wilson and I know that's a stupid thing to even think right now, but it's how I feel. Heartbroken over something I lost years ago.

I clear my throat. "The sun will come up soon." I look at my watch.

"What are we going to do?" she asks, biting her bottom lip.

And just like that, reality sets in. Our situation is thrown back in my face.

The way she asks me…*what are we going to do?* She is truly asking. She's looking to me for an answer. She's worried.

Truthfully, I'd be lying if I said I wasn't. I'm not my best. Any other day, if he didn't jump me from behind, I could take Trig's crazy ass with no problem, but I'm weak, malnourished. I'm doing good just to stand up right now.

And talking about our past hasn't really helped, but I have an instinct to protect her. So, when the time comes, that's what I'll do. No matter if it gets me killed. She gives me the energy I need. She has to run, though, as quickly as she can.

"We're gonna fight, love. Because that's the only choice we have."

She nods. "Have you thought more about why you think he's doing this to us?"

I shake my head. "That's all I've thought about. I just can't wrap my head around it. I keep going over all the shit I've done and how it would have affected him. How have I taken everything from the man when I've never known him to have a goddamn thing? He was a foster kid, just like Sweep...Johnny," I say, correcting myself. "He didn't have a family when I met him. I don't understand what the hell he's talking..."

I stop mid-sentence, my mind churning rapidly. I grab my hand, feeling for the ring.

I had it on the day he took us. I know I did.

I plan to take everything from you.

Memories come flooding back from right before all of this happened. I remember the note left at the shop.

An eye for an eye.

I'll take everything you love first.

And then I'm coming for you.

I remember the conversation with Moretti before the funeral. Trig must have hit me so hard it wiped my memory out. I must have had a concussion and it's all coming back to me now. Once, when we were kids, Paul wrecked on a dirt bike he'd stolen from some rich kid.

He hit his head; blood was everywhere. He was talking nonsense and couldn't remember a damn thing. Doc said he suffered a major concussion, that one day out of the blue he might remember what happened or he might never. This must be what I'm experiencing.

Thinking about Paul has me thinking about my plan. Everything comes back to me. Every single thing.

"What?" she asks.

"Dear God," I say, looking back up at her. "I killed his whole family."

Chapter Thirty-Three

Bones
2019

Hours went by before she stopped crying and I know listening to her was what I deserved. It's my own personal nightmare. I've already got a seat reserved for me in Hell, but this…what I've done, it ratifies it and the note in my pocket seals the deal. I went back to the shop after I was sure she'd fallen asleep and what I found…she'll never forgive me.

I sit outside A-Street Flower Shop, looking at the building from the outside as I smoke. It's late, but a few cars pass, checking out the place, wondering what happened, not knowing that only hours ago, my little brother was gunned down and the woman I love was almost taken from me.

I open my car door, stepping out, exhaling smoke into the air. Looking around, I walk across the road, lifting the yellow tape, stepping over broken glass. I walk inside, checking out the destruction left behind, my mind reeling. Blood dries on the floor, and flowers hang in broken pots.

I have a lot of enemies; some I don't even know about. This was always in the back of my mind. This was my worst fear that my actions would cause someone I loved to get hurt. I'm a monster, but even monsters care about something.

Family has always been important to me. Ma and my brothers, Bexley, Sweep, and Trig are the pieces that hold my life's puzzle together.

Now a piece of that is gone.

And I'm fucking furious.

Anger and hurt collide in my chest, like two fighting demons. I scan the place and my madness grows at what was done here.

They have no idea who they just fucked with. My hands shake. I lift up the table nearest me, along with the chair beside it, tossing them across the room. My hands hang on my hips and I bow my head, running my fingers over my jaw as my eyes land on a bottle.

My eyes narrow. I reach down and pick it up, noticing the piece of paper inside of it. I tip it upside down and dig the paper out.

The sound of the record player switching songs brings me back to the present. I hold the paper in my hand as I sit at the bar. Whoever did this is not so bright. What criminal leaves a note at a crime scene for the police to find? Of course, the police didn't find it. I did and it's clear that I'm who it was meant for. We pay the cops off, so eventually this would have been brought to my attention, and something tells me whoever did this knew that. It's too bad that while they were writing this out, they probably failed to think that they were, in fact, writing out their own death certificate.

My eyes go to the ceiling and I think about Bexley up there sleeping in my bed as I take a sip of my drink. God, how much I've wanted her in my bed, but not like this. I didn't want her heartbroken, under my covers, clutching onto her husband's wedding band. I didn't want my brother to die.

It's a sad reality, and what's even sadder is I hate how much she misses him. I'm a piece of shit, but I've never pretended to be anything better. I am who I am, and I make no apologies for it.

I get why she didn't want to stay in their house, but my brother wouldn't be happy about her being here and I think that's why she was hesitant.

She's more unavailable now than she's ever been, and that's a decision she clearly made. She killed me on the spot when she said she didn't need me. I guess in the back of my fucked-up mind, I always thought she *did*.

Or maybe it was me who needed her.

Bexley and I have always had this fire between us. A light simmer when we were kids, and then when she came back that Thanksgiving, man, what a time we had together. I never thought our lives would turn out the way they did.

I lift the necklace I have around my neck, playing with the knot that binds us. She'll never forgive me, and I don't ever expect her to. I hit my smoke, twirling my glass on the bar. The door opens behind me and I turn to see Sweep.

Goosebumps appear on my bare back before the door shuts. I exhale, looking in front of me, watching the smoke twirl in the air. He takes a seat and I slide the note over for him to read as I sip my drink, feeling the sting from the whiskey all the way down.

I run a hand over the small bit of hair on my chest. The cigarillo hangs from my lips, and I wipe condensation from my glass.

He tosses the note away from his hand. "Fucking hell, Bones," he says, shaking his head.

I nod, taking a drag from my smoke. "Fucking hell, brother."

Chapter Thirty-Four

Bexley
One month three days missing

"What? You killed his whole family and you are just now remembering that? Are you kidding me right now?" I watch him as he stands across the room not saying anything. "Danny, you gotta talk to me here. I mean, Jesus Christ."

His eyes go to mine. "I've never killed anyone who didn't deserve it."

"Do you hear yourself? Oh my God. Who am I locked in this shack with?" I run my hands through my hair, gripping at the ends in disbelief.

"You've got this wrong," he says.

I nod my head quickly. "Explain then."

"I was a kid. I didn't realize who I was talking to. I thought I was being questioned by the police, but they were working for Moretti. You know how many times I've told you the cops around here are dirty."

"I know."

"They told Moretti what I said. They told him who I described, and he put out a hit."

I feel my brow furrow. "So, he had the people killed that murdered your mom and dad?"

He shakes his head. "He had his whole family killed, Bex. Carson was the only survivor. The ring I wear… it had to have been his dad's. Moretti sent it to me in a teddy bear. It was still on his finger."

"Hold on." I put my hand up. "You mean that man sent you someone's finger in a teddy bear?"

"Yeah," he says, like that's exactly what he did. Like that's normal in his world.

I can't wrap my head around this. "He said he was going to take everything from you."

He nods. "Just like I did him. The day he killed Samuel, he tossed a bottle into the shop. I went back and got it. It said an eye for an eye. I'll take everything you love first and then I'm coming for you."

I remember the bottle and the note. I was going back to get it when I ran a red light and nearly got killed. I was also going to get it before Carson grabbed us. I would have known for sure this was because of Danny if I had found it before him.

"So, this whole time you knew this was because of you and you lied to me about it."

"I didn't remember. It's all coming back to me. I don't know how I forgot all of this." He rubs his head, looking confused and concerned. I take pity on him.

"You were hit hard. And he was drugging us at first. It's understandable." This is all crazy. Danny was just a boy. I mean, how was he supposed to know about bad guys paying off cops and the crooked way of the world?

"This isn't your fault, Danny. You were just a kid. But, how have you not known you've been hanging around a psychopath?"

He scoffs. "I did know. I just didn't realize he could turn on me like this." He thinks for a moment. "You know it doesn't matter what the facts are. He only sees it one way. He blames me for everything that happened to him.

"And now Samuel is gone, but he was trying to get to you because he knows how much I love you. How could I not have seen this? He's been acting odd lately, the rubber band popping when it was just him, Sweep, and I. I questioned it out loud to him and Sweep. I even said, 'There are only so many people who know about mine and Bexley's history.' And there he was sitting in the backseat, knowing it was him the whole time. Goddammit.

"He's a fucking traitor. He's gone against me, his authority, his brother."

I watch Danny as his back straightens and he looks out the window as the sun starts to rise.

"He will die. I will avenge Samuel's death. I will slit Trig's fucking throat and stare into his eyes as he bleeds out. Mark me."

Chapter Thirty-Five

Bexley
2019

I wake and a wrecking ball of pain hits me in the gut. Jumping up, I fly to the bathrocm and puke. I sit back against the tub after I flush the toilet and the tears fall. I put my face in my hands, coughing and wiping down my cheeks, looking to the ceiling for some answers. It's only been hours since I lost Samuel. Only a short time since I watched him leave me.

He sounded so scared, so childlike. His words keep replaying in my mind.

"I don't want to die."

And I just sat there, lying to him. Telling him he was going to be okay. Telling him bullshit.

I stare down at the floor, void of energy, but knowing there are things I have to get done.

I look to the watch on my wrist. It's morning, but Danny's blacked-out curtains don't let the sun through. The sun could never shine again, and I'd be okay with it.

There's no controlling grief. It'll go when it decides to. I learned that from Mama's death.

I loved Samuel in my own way. He was my best friend, and watching someone die in front of you, who was such an important part of your life…there's no getting over that.

Regardless, I can't sit here and let it consume me. Not yet anyway. I have a funeral to plan and I've got to find that bottle.

I reach for the sink and pull myself up, looking at my reflection in the mirror. Redness lines my eyes, and they're swollen. I cup my hands and let them fill with water. I splash my face.

Grabbing my toothbrush, I attempt to clean my teeth and then throw my beanie back over my head, wishing I'd brought my shades. I'd like to make zero eye contact today. I take off Samuel's shirt, place it back into the bag, and slide on some jeans and my Tracers, along with a long-sleeved tee and my long coat.

I look in the mirror a second time, swallow the tears back that won't seem to stop, and turn to walk out of the room.

Looking over at the dresser, I see a pair of Ray-Bans. I snatch them up, along with my purse and phone.

I walk down the stairs and take in the few people who are already at the bar this early in the morning. Some have coffee; some have a beer.

"Good morning," Mae says to me from behind the bar. "Can I get you some coffee?"

"Please," I say, walking up. "Where's Danny?"

She turns to look my way as she fills up a cup. "He and the boys went out."

I nod, wondering what that means exactly.

"Cream?" she asks.

I shake my head, bringing the cup to my lips.

"I'm sorry about Samuel," she says sadly.

I look at her for a moment, hearing her words. How many people will say that to me over the next few weeks, months, hell, even years? I'm a widow now. I'm too young to be a widow.

Mae's got blonde dreads and wears black-framed glasses. She's got a sleeve of tattoos and fire red lips. She fits in here. I feel like I stand out like a sore thumb.

"Thanks." I look up at the TV and see the news is on. They're covering the shop.

"A young man was gunned down yesterday evening at A-Street Flower Shop and the police are questioning if it's gang-related," the news reporter says.

My heart drops. The camera moves from her to the shop and I get to see the damage in daylight.

Jesus. The windows are completely gone. Dirt and glass are everywhere on the inside.

"We'll update you on the story with the news at six." The TV goes to commercial and I look down at my coffee. A tear falls and I cover my mouth as I try to contain it.

"Hey," Mae says. "Give me that cup." She grabs the cup, pouring a splash of whiskey in it, then she slides it back to me.

"Thank you," I say, wiping my eyes behind the sunglasses.

"No problem. You need some food. Want me to order some?"

"I can't eat," I say, taking a sip of the coffee.

She nods in understanding.

I grab my phone from my back pocket. I unlock the screen and see a text.

Didn't want to wake you. The boys and I had to go out. Don't leave the bar. If you need anything, Mae will get it.

I exhale and drop the phone. Great, I'm stuck here. This is why I got away from the south side. But it didn't matter. The bad found me, and it took Samuel. It ruined Billie's shop and it has me hiding in a bar. I rub my forehead, then bring my drink to my lips, wondering what the hell to do.

Mae walks up to me. "Want me to turn this crap off?" she asks.

I shake my head. "Won't change anything."

She nods, wiping the bar, and I can tell she's thinking something.

I've never really been around her much, but she's worked for Danny for a long time now. My mind is a stupid thing and it goes to places that are so unimportant.

But I can't help it.

Have they slept together?

Does he care about her?

"He still loves you, you know," she says.

I don't respond, completely thrown off.

She smiles, but it's laced with hurt. "Sometimes when he sits here, I can just tell he's thinking about you, wondering what you're doing, if you're happy." She shrugs. "I'm here. Every day, every night," she emphasizes the last words. I feel my eye twitch. "And all he cares about is you."

I don't look away from her, glad I have the shades on. This woman is hurting. God, how I know what it feels like to be hurt by Danny.

"And yet you have him," I say.

She swallows, and her eyes fill with tears. "But do you know what it's like to be with someone who'd rather be with someone else? Do you know what it's like to love someone who can only give you a small piece of them? You have all of his memories. His past."

I think about Samuel, wondering if he had someone to talk to, would he say the same thing as Mae about our marriage?

I lift my chin slightly. "And you have his future."

Chapter Thirty-Six

Bones
One month three days missing

The sun comes up, blanketing us with its warm golden light, filling the cabin with a false sense of hope. Bexley's speculated this whole time that this was somehow my fault, and now we've confirmed it.

I turn toward the window, looking for his truck. Waiting.

I hold on to a piece of sharp glass from the window we broke with my chair on the other side of the cabin. My shirt is wrapped around it, but one wrong move and I can cut myself severely.

"Danny, I'm sorry for the things I've said. I know this isn't your fault now."

I give her a reassuring smile, happy she thinks that, but I still blame me. "It's okay, love. No man is wise at all times."

She smirks. "You and your Irish sayings." She laughs lightly. "Your dad would be proud," she says. "You didn't let his Irish background die with him."

I flinch at the compliment. "I learned everything from him," I say, clearing my throat.

Her smile fades as she swallows. "Danny, I…" She looks into my eyes and I look into hers, and in this moment we share an understanding.

"I know, Bex. Me too."

Chapter Thirty-Seven

Bones
2019

We had businesses to collect money from this morning and that didn't go smoothly. I let some druggie borrow a couple grand to start up a new restaurant and things aren't going well. He's getting high in the kitchen he's serving food from, he's in a mess with the health department, and he's not making his payments. So, I had to get my hands bloody.

"What did I tell you, Miles?" I ask as I slam my fist into the man's face. "Repeat what I said."

Miles spits onto the floor, wiggling his hands, which are tied behind his back.

"You said I'd be okay if I paid at the end of the month."

"And what day is it?"

"Bones, it's only the first. It's only a day late."

Another punch to the face.

"Nope. It's eleven days late from the original pay date. I gave you ten extra days, Miles. Ten whole days. I thought that was kind of me. I thought I was doing you a favor."

I lean down so I can look Miles in his battered face. "I find out you're snorting coccine next to the food you're preparing. I find out you're drinking on the job. This isn't good for business and you know what they say?"

He shakes his head.

"They say, you must crack the nuts before you can eat the kernel."

Miles looks confused.

Sweep chimes in, "Success takes hard work."

"Exactly. Sweep took the words right out of my mouth. You must do better. People are hearing about your bad habits and you know what it's doing to me?"

Miles doesn't say anything.

"It wasn't a rhetorical question, Miles. I need you to answer."

"It makes you look bad," he mumbles.

"What was that?" I ask. I look over at Trig, who's popping his rubber band. Miles looks over at him, too, nervously.

"Did you hear that, Trig?"

Trig nods his head, looking pissed, looking uneasy.

I look back at Miles, "I said it makes you look bad," he repeats. Sweep leans against the counter with his ankles crossed, looking unenthused as usual.

"I'm sorry, Bones. I'll do better. I got a little bit of money in the office. I can give you that now and give you the other next week." Miles looks back at Trig again. "Why...why is he popping that rubber band?"

"Therapy," Trig says.

"Keeps him from shooting people in the face," Sweep says evenly.

I exhale, grabbing my knife from my waist to cut the zip tie. "Go get the money."

Miles only gave me half, which didn't please me. I'll be back next week to collect the rest, and if he doesn't have it for me, he'll lose a finger.

I didn't want to deal with this shit today. I wanted business to go smoothly so I could get back home and help Bexley with the funeral arrangements. I wanted to be there for her. I know she's still at the bar because I've got men watching it.

Mae texted me earlier and let me know Bex was up. She also told me she gave her some spiked coffee. Said she didn't look well and didn't seem happy at all that she was stuck there all day.

But it is what it is. All I care about is her safety right now and I couldn't stay with her all day. I have a job to do and I need to talk to Moretti.

I look down at the note in my hand.

An eye for an eye.

I'll take everything you love first.
And then I'm coming for you.

"Who the fuck is this, anyway? I ask.

"Seems like someone's after you," Trig says from the back.

"Well, if that ain't obvious as fuck," I say, tossing the note onto the dash.

"What did you do, Bones?" Trig says.

"If I knew, do you think I would be questioning what this is? What the hell's wrong with you lately?" I look back at him.

He shrugs. "Just tired. Stayed up too late with a girl."

"You need to leave those whores at the clubhouse alone. Thought you would have learned your lesson when you were dealing with that stalker bitch before Mickey got killed."

"Yeah, well, I guess I didn't." He starts popping his rubber band. I look over at Sweep questionably.

He shakes his head, like he has no idea what's up with this crazy fuck either. I ignore it. I've got too much on my mind. I need to know who the hell killed my little brother. I need to know why they went to Bexley's work. They were clearly after her to hurt me.

But who all knows about our past? Could Moretti have done this? Is he trying to get rid of me?

But that doesn't make sense. How have I taken anything from Moretti? If anything, I've handed him the fucking world without him having to lift so much as a finger. But he did warn me to stay away from her. Maybe he knew I was keeping an eye on her, and maybe he thought it was distracting me.

I'm going in circles here.

I've got to figure out what Moretti and Nugget are doing. I need to dig into that more. Once I find out who did this, though, I swear they'll suffer. They think I've taken everything from them…just fucking wait.

"What the hell happened to you?" Moretti asks as we walk into his office.

"I hit something," I say. "Get me a towel," I say to Nugget who stands at the door.

I hear his protest through his heavy exhale. I take a seat as Trig and Sweep sit behind me. I'm wired, and I slept like shit last night. Guilt swims in my bloodstream like a heavy dose of cocaine, and it's messing with me.

"You doing okay?" Moretti asks as Nugget tosses me the towel, nearly hitting me in the face.

"You motherfucker." I stand up, walking over to him, when Sweep grabs my arm.

"Stop, it," Moretti says. "Nugget, get out. Jesus Christ, you two."

I wrap the towel around my battered-up fist. pointing to Nugget's back as I look at Moretti. "Why do you still let that piece of shit come around?"

"Shut up. Sit down," he says to me.

I feel my jaw tighten, but I take my seat.

"What do we know?" he asks me.

"Whoever killed Samuel left me a note."

"A note?" he questions.

"Yeah. An eye for an eye. Says they'll take everything from me, just like I did them."

Moretti narrows his eyes. "So, this is retaliation."

"Apparently."

He nods, sitting back in his chair. "Whoever this was, was after the girl, though, right?"

"They shot up her work. I'm guessing Samuel wasn't the main target. At least not right then." I don't bring up the fact I think he might have something to do with it. That wouldn't be smart.

"Why don't you lay low for a while. Let me do some talking. Figure some stuff out. Atlanta needs checking up on anyway. Take the girl, and those two. Get out of town for a bit."

"What about my family?" Why does he want me out of town? Is it because of him and Nugget's new partnership? They want me out of the way?

I'm fishing, but I can't help it. I'm just trying to grab onto some reasonable idea of why someone would want her dead. He's probably just thinking I need to get away so I don't get shot while riding down the street. Fuck, I don't know. I shouldn't doubt the man. He's been there for me since I was a kid. He's given me no reason to think he would have done this.

"Your brother's the mayor. He'll be fine and I'll have men watching Ma for you."

"All right," I reply. But I'll feel better once I talk to Paul. "We gotta bury Samuel and then we'll be on our way."

"Take the private jet," Moretti says.

"'Preciate it," I reply.

Sweep grabs his smokes and flips his Zippo open as we three pull up to my bar.

"We'll organize Samuel's funeral. Have it tomorrow," I tell him and Trig. "Whoever is after me won't know about Atlanta. I don't know what I did to this motherfucker, but they're going to be sorry. Right now, I need to make sure Bexley is safe, so we need distance from Postings."

"Yeah," Sweep agrees. "It's obvious she was the target."

"There's just not too many people who know about our history. I'm drawing a blank at who could have done this."

"Me too," he says.

"I need to go speak with Paul. I'll be back in a little while."

Sweep nods and he and Trig exit the car. I grab my cell and call the mayor of Posting.

"Danny," he answers.

"Hey," I respond, sounding just as weary as he does. "Can you meet me? Can we talk?"

"Where?"

"Biagio's." I haven't eaten and they have private areas where we can speak confidentially.

"Be there in ten," he says.

Once I pull up to the restaurant, the valet takes my keys and I head upstairs. In a gray, single-breasted suit, Paul is seated in the back close to the window. Biagio's is on the north side of town. It's upscale and dark. He stands when I near. I give him a nod, removing my coat and placing it over the back of the vinyl dining chair. They offered to check it at the door, but I waved them off.

"I assumed you'd prefer a scotch," he says, returning to his seat.

"You assumed right," I reply, taking my seat and lifting my glass. Ice clinks against the side as I taste a sip. I lick my lips, savoring the bold warmth of the Dalmore.

"How are you holding up?" he asks me.

"Not well. You?"

He shakes his head, looking grave. "Heartbroken. I all but raised Samuel. It almost feels as if I've lost a son."

I look out the window at the cars' taillights below us. "I'm sorry," I tell him.

"Oh, but you've lost someone, too. For that I am also sorry. Grief is heavy. How's Bexley?"

"Same as us." I clear my throat, wiping my hand on my slacks.

The waiter walks up and I order a steak, medium rare, with roasted potatoes. Paul has the same. Once the waiter leaves us, I exhale and grab the note from my pocket before placing it on the table. Paul's eyes jump down to it before looking back at me.

"Do I want to know what that says?" he questions.

"No, but you need to anyway."

He lifts his brow and reaches for the note. I watch his eyes bounce over the words and then he tosses it back on the table. He takes a drink from his glass, chewing on his inner cheek. "Where did you get this?"

"The shop. Either it was thrown in there or placed. I'm not sure."

"The bullets were meant for Bexley," he says.

"Yes."

"They were trying to hurt you by killing her," he says.

"Yes."

He doesn't say anything else. We sit in silence, and moments later our food is brought to us. I cut into my steak and take a bite. I eat one potato and that's all I can stomach. Paul doesn't touch his.

I've been working out a plan in my mind for years on how I wanted my life to eventually end up. I've been trying to figure out a way to get my woman back and live a good life with her.

Did I want my brother to die for this to happen? No, of course not. I knew eventually Bexley would realize that she wasn't happy and her life wasn't fulfilled. She would leave him and hopefully he'd meet someone else. Am I being presumptuous?

No.

My confidence in what we shared has never wavered. Was I disappointed when she chose to marry Samuel? Yes. But still, I knew her feelings for me ran deeper than anyone else could touch.

Things worked out differently than I had hoped and I'm heartbroken about it. But there's no changing it, so forward is where we go.

"I'm not sure what to feel right now," he says. "Being angry with you won't get me anywhere. It won't bring back Samuel."

I scrub a hand down my mouth.

"He was one of the good ones," Paul says.

"That he was," I agree. I run my finger over my fork.

Paul looks at me. "Do you have any idea who did this?"

"No. I've never been more clueless."

He nods. "They'll be coming after all of us then."

"They will. I need you to up security, Paul. Make sure Ma is protected, too. I'll have my own people watching her, but I need to know you have people, too."

"That's not an issue," he says.

I hold my glass up for a refill. Moments later, I have one placed on the table.

"What about you?" Paul asks.

I take a sip of my drink, and then I grab my case of smokes from inside my blazer's pocket. Knowing they won't say anything to me about it, I light one. I toss the silver case onto the table. "I have a plan, brother. It's a hell of one." I blow smoke from my lungs and lift my glass. "I'm going to need your help."

Chapter Thirty-Eight

Trig

I stand against the kitchen counter when he walks in. "You killed his fucking brother."

"How the hell was I supposed to know he would be there?"

I shake my head, hitting my cigarette.

"Weren't you going to do it, anyway?" he asks.

I nod. "True." I pick up my beer and take a sip.

"What's the plan now?" he asks.

"They've planned for us to head to Atlanta tomorrow night. But we're not going to Atlanta. I've just got to figure out a way to get Bones away from Sweep. Keep your phone on. I'll call you when it's time."

Chapter Thirty-Nine

Bexley
One month three days missing

"When he shows up, I need you to run as fast as you can to that truck. He never turns it off, so the keys will be in it. Go and then look for a phone. He might have left one in there."

"I don't want to leave you. I can help."

"No, love. I need to know you're out of harm's way. Please do this for me."

Tears fill my eyes when I know they shouldn't. I shouldn't care for this man. I should be glad he's giving me an easy out, but just thinking about him trying to fight Carson by himself... He's too weak. How will he win? My eyes move from the wrapped glass that sits in the chair before going back to him.

Wrinkles run across his forehead, a scar cuts through his left eyebrow. I wonder how he got it. I look at his full lips and his beard that has a strand or two of gray.

I suddenly grow panicked, like if I don't make a move here, I'll never have a chance again.

Without overthinking, I reach my hand out and grip the back of his neck. His eyes bounce to mine. He freezes, making sure this is okay, but I started it.

I want it. I don't want to think about who I'll hurt, who I love, and what this means. I want to kiss Danny and so I do. My lips touch his.

There are many types of kisses. Kisses in hello, kisses in goodbye, kisses that are sweet and slow, and some that are quick and over. This one is different from any of those. It's like tectonic plates colliding, forming something bigger than all of us. Mountains, earthquakes.

It's painful, yet there's so much pleasure, I could die. Danny's hand circles my neck. I feel his thick fingers wrap around me, gently, carefully. His tongue slides past my lips, and I feel like I've been away from home for decades, and now, finally, I'm back. I feel the tears fall down my cheeks. I squeeze my eyes shut, holding on to his arms.

Danny wraps one behind my back, pulling me nearer to him. Like he can't have me close enough. Like he wants my body to melt into his. And it does. It caves, it gives, it remembers, wondering how it ever forgot what this feels like with him.

How right we are for one another. His breath tastes stale, and I'm sure mine is awful, but passion overrides things like that. It forgives the unpleasantness in the moment and focuses on the beautiful.

Oh, how beautiful.

Danny pulls away, placing his forehead on mine. His eyes look through me.

And that's when I feel it. He's shaking.

"I'm sorry," he whispers. His voice is hoarse. "I shouldn't have done that."

"You didn't. I did."

That's when he smirks. It's faint, but I see it. I reach up and run my finger along the scar on his eyebrow after he breaks away from my forehead. He licks his lips. He swallows. The tattoos on his neck move.

"Promise me," he says.

And I know what he's referring to. "I'll run."

But I know I won't. I'm lying. I will fight beside him. I will make sure he is safe, just like I know he will make sure I am.

Chapter Forty

Bexley
2019

I sit by the window with the curtain pulled back so I can see out into the street. I rest my jaw on my bent knees as I run my finger over Samuel's wedding band. Dusk flirts with night while I look out at the jagged skyline in the distance. My stomach growls, reminding me that I haven't eaten, and then my gut twists at the thought of trying.

I don't pretend to sit here and act like Samuel and I had the perfect marriage.

What is that, anyway?

There were moments of doubt and times we didn't see eye to eye. I exhale, dropping the ring around my neck. I've always loved two men, but regardless of the love I've felt for Danny, I wouldn't have hurt Samuel. I wouldn't have acted on my feelings for Danny. I know Samuel had his suspicions of us, and that part eats me up inside. Samuel never knew that I knew Danny first. Samuel never knew that I've kept a secret this long.

There's a small voice in my mind. It's way back in a special place we all keep our darkest secrets. The ones we don't share with anyone else.

Insurgent

Maybe we're too afraid of the judgment we might receive, or we just don't want to admit it to ourselves. But that voice tells me that part of the reason I chose Samuel was because I knew Danny would never be available the way I needed him to be. I knew Danny could never lead a normal life.

Birds soar over the businesses across the street and I see the man who owns the Laundromat come out with a bag of trash.

Next door is a small bakery. It's been there since I was a girl, and beside that is a store where you can buy lottery tickets and whatever little thing you may have forgotten at the big chain store a few miles from here.

This neighborhood will always hold the sense of home for me. I ran these streets with the boys, but it's not a safe place. At night, the monsters come out. They vandalize buildings and break windows. They rob people and steal, but I think I know why none of these locally owned places are touched. And I'm pretty sure it's because of Danny. One of his Irish sayings passes through my mind.

Even black hens lay white eggs.

Maybe the big bad wolf isn't so bad, or maybe he is. The door behind me opens and I twist in my chair, holding on to my knees still. *Speaking of the wolf.*

"Hey," Danny says.

"Where have you been all day?"

Danny shuts the door, dropping his phone on the table. "I had some business to take care of." He rubs his eyes and pops his neck.

I narrow my eyes. "Whatever that means."

He exhales.

"Can you tell me why I've been stuck here all day?"

"Oh, I don't know, Bexley. Maybe because someone is trying to kill you."

"There he is," I say.

"What are you talking about now?"

"The asshole who's Danny O'Brien. My husband just died, and you leave me here in this dump all day, not knowing anything, not having anyone to talk to."

"Don't talk down about my place, and Mae is downstairs if you wanted to talk to someone."

"You're such an idiot, Danny. The woman is in love with you. I'm the last person she wants to have a conversation with."

He stops, removes his watch, and looks at me. "Why would she feel any certain way toward you?"

"Why wouldn't she?" I ask.

"I really don't know, Bexley."

I shake my head, looking back out the window. I hear the clink of his watch and then his wallet hits the dresser along with some change.

"How long have you been seeing her?" I ask, not looking over at him, but in my peripheral I can see him remove his shirt before he takes a seat on the bed.

"Years," he says.

I keep my eyes focused on the evening sky. "Do you love her?" I'm inquiring about something that may hurt me. Flaw of being human.

I look back, because I need to see his facial expression. He rubs a hand over his five o'clock shadow and the light reflects off a black diamond ring I've never noticed before. His hands are fully tattooed, showing a skeleton as if it's his own. It's 3D. My eyes go to the necklace he wears, just like I still wear the bracelet he gifted me.

Samuel questioned this bracelet one time and I lied and told him it was a gift from my mother.

"Do I love her?" he asks. He lifts a brow, shaking his head slightly. "What do you mean by that? Do I love her the way you love Samuel or the way I love you?"

I don't respond. Instead, I look away again.

"Nothing?" he says. "You ask that from me and then you have nothing to say?"

"What am I supposed to say?"

"Just tell me the truth. All I want is the truth from you."

"What truth do you want?"

He stands up and walks over to me. Reaching down, he grabs my arm. "This truth. You still wear my bracelet after all this time. Why?"

I look at my wrist before looking at the necklace that resembles it. "And you still wear that. There's your truth. No matter what we do...where we go, we can't rid ourselves of the past. It follows like an unwanted shadow." I see his busted knuckles, and once again I'm reminded of the monster he is.

"Is it that unwanted?" he asks, and I feel his thumb brush against my wrist. My eyes shoot to his before going to his bare chest, the ink on his skin, and the muscles under them. Once upon a time, I would have relished in his touch. Bathed in it, like the summertime sun.

But I don't know this man anymore. I yank my hand away. "Yes. It's that unwanted." I look toward the window, and he inhales.

"Noted," he says. "I won't touch you again. Have you eaten?"

"No," I reply.

"You will eat. I can't have you wasting away on me, no matter how much you want to. We have to plan Samuel's funeral and have it tomorrow evening and then we've got to get out of town."

"What?" I say as he walks to the bathroom.

"I'll have Mae grab you some food. I'm getting a shower."

"Have you no compassion?" I ask him. "How can you ask her to do that? Have you fucked her in here? In this bed?"

He turns around. "Where else would I fuck her, Bex? Did you think my life stopped because you left it?"

I narrow my eyes.

"Do you think this has all been a walk in the park for me?" He slaps his chest. "You are a piece of work, girl. Of all the men you could have picked, you picked him. *My brother.* I told you to stay away from him. Remember? I asked you to leave him be when I saw those text messages you two were sending on the phone I bought you. You might as well have stabbed me in the goddamn chest."

I grip the back of the chair. "Oh, I love how even after all this time, you think you can control me. The phone you bought me. You told me to stay away from him. You act as though I went after him as soon as you were handcuffed and taken to jail. You did this, you know?

"You were the no-show. You might as well have pushed me into his arms yourself."

He lifts his chin. "Yeah, maybe I did. But you didn't put up a fight."

"Screw you, Danny." I stand up and walk to the door.

"Where you going?"

"This fucking room is too small for the both of us." And with that, I walk out.

Chapter Forty-One

Bones
One month three days missing

I'm shaking. Trembling noticeably, because I'm touching her, because she's letting me and not acting as though I'm disgusting. I don't want to let her go. Ever. Afraid that if I do, she'll never allow me to do this again. Can she feel how right we are together? How it's this easy. We're older now. Wiser, more experienced. I'd like to see how she looks under those clothes, how her body has changed.

I'm sure it's magnificent. But this isn't the place for that sort of thing. We're in danger. I'm not well, and she's probably not thinking clearly. Facing death isn't something I'm unaccustomed to. I've seen it, I've delivered it. But standing here with her as she promises she'll run…it's not the same.

I may die.

I may never see her again and I may never get the chance to make things right with us.

I have a plan, but now I'm not sure if I will ever be able to see it through.

I'm not strong.

I'm the weakest I've ever been.

Paige P. Horne

This will end in death.
But will it be his or mine?

Chapter Forty-Two

Bones
2019

I run my hand over the fogged mirror, revealing a man's face I don't recognize sometimes. I don't know why, but my mind goes to Bryce Grant, the ex-club owner who lives in Atlanta. We went down there and took everything he'd built. Something he worked his whole life for. We made him see he had no way out of the situation he was in. The boy was about to do some hard time for illegal gambling and a few other serious charges.

I used that against him. I also used the woman he loves. But Bryce took it differently than most men who'd built a kingdom on their own only for someone to snatch it away from them.

And that's probably because of the woman he has. He has someone to be better for.

I think about how his life is clean now and void of the shit that comes along with all of this.

Samuel's death is on me, and it's a heavy weight.

The heaviest.

Paige P. Horne

The last conversation we had wasn't pleasant. I told him to get the fuck out of my face. I wish it wouldn't have been that way. I have so much regret now, it's eating me up inside. I feel the beat of my heart, the small thump in my chest, letting me know that I am only human, and humans are a complicated, messed-up species.

I grip the porcelain, looking down, clenching my teeth. I breathe deeply, clearing my mind from stupid thoughts. What is done is done. I hear my father's voice. *"Hindsight is the best insight to foresight."*

I look back at myself, lifting my chin and straightening my back, and then I smash the mirror with my fist.

Chapter Forty-Three

Bexley
One month three days missing

We stand together for what seems like hours, but I know it's only minutes at best before I pull away. He acts as if he doesn't want me to, like he's scared to death that I'll disappear right before his eyes and he'll never see me again.

It's not easy to have a love like this. It's not a clean love, like what Samuel and I shared.

Samuel.

How could you kiss Danny when Samuel's only been gone for a month?

I shake that thought, but it makes me put more distance between Danny and me. Our love is dirty, messy. Risky. Now is not the time for lust and all that comes with it.

We don't know when Carson is coming, but he usually does every few days so we're prepared… well, as prepared as we can be. I'm sick with worry. I see the fight in Danny's eyes. The darkness that lives inside of him shines brightly. He's ready to do this. But am I ready?

What will happen?

If we do live through this, will we go on about our lives as if we didn't share this horrible experience? Should I move on and try to live a normal life?

How?

What will he do?

Where will I go?

So many questions and zero answers.

I think about a conversation we had days ago.

"Promise me."

"Promise what?"

"That when we get out of here, you'll go after it. That you'll leave this town and never look back."

Danny looked sickly then, and he doesn't look much better now. He's only human. That's easy to forget sometimes, looking at him. So sure of himself, so wise in some ways, and shake worthy stupid in others. He could have had it all with me. We could have had it all, but he chose a path I couldn't follow.

Will he continue to go alone, or will we come together after all of this?

I feel I have my answer. I've already promised him, after all. That kiss didn't mean anything; it was just something two people do when they're put in a situation like we've been put into. It was right to do at the time, but it won't happen again.

Chapter Forty-Four

Bexley
2019

The morning comes and we wake like robots. We dress, climb into the car, and plan Samuel's funeral. I nod yes to this and yes to that. Point to the things I want and shake my head when I don't approve of something. By late afternoon, with the demands coming from Danny for things to hurry along, we all stand outside by Samuel's casket.

There will be no Catholic funeral for my husband, which confuses Ma, but with a little pep talk from Danny, she lets it go.

Regardless, I know how much he loved Ireland and his Irish background just as Paul and Danny do, so I insisted on that to be present and I got no argument from anyone.

The snow begins to fall as tears roll down my face. Ma holds on to my arm, dabbing her nose with a tissue. Paul stands tall, holding his hands in front of him, his wife by his side, his children's hands in hers. Danny and Johnny stand together across from me as the priest begins to pray.

"May the Irish hills caress you.

May her lakes and rivers bless you.

May the luck of the Irish enfold you. May the blessings of Saint Patrick behold you."

During the prayer, my eyes drift from the snow-sprinkled ground to Samuel's casket with its simple red roses. That's how Samuel was.

Simple.

Easy.

"Wait," a kid yells. "Can you grab it?" he says as the ball rolls past me. In heels that aren't fit to run in, I jog, trying to reach down and grab the ball, when someone scoops it up. I look up, my hair in my face. I blow it out, seeing a smile that makes my heart skip.

"Hey," Samuel says, tossing the ball back to the kid.

"Thanks," the kid says before he runs off.

"Hey," I say, standing up straight, slightly out of breath, and not just from going after the ball.

The summer sun shines upon his face, showing gold flecks in his eyes that I remember seeing when we were kids.

"How are you?" he says.

I nod, sliding a piece of hair behind my ear. "Fine."

"Just fine?" He smiles.

I shrug. "Just fine."

We stare at each other for a moment and time seems to stop, but the world keeps going on around us. He's tan and got this shadow of a beard. He seems older, but not much. It's been what? Only two years since I last saw him on this very street, changing my tire in the pouring rain. He looks so good, though.

"You seeing anyone?" he asks.

I shake my head. "No."

"You want to?"

I smile, feeling myself blush. Who is this guy, and where did shy Samuel go?

"I don't know."

He looks at his watch and then back up at me. "Come to dinner with me. I'll help you make your mind up."

I bite my lip, feeling something I haven't in a long time. Excited, nervous.

"Okay," I say.

I jump when someone touches my shoulder.

"We need to go," Danny says. Reality slams into my chest like a bullet, breaking skin and blood vessels. I cry for Samuel because he didn't deserve this. He had friends, he had a good life, and this funeral does not celebrate the man who was better than all of this.

After we say our goodbyes to Paul and Ma, we climb into the car. Danny and I sit in the back and Johnny drives. We move through the cemetery with slow ease and I find myself growing so angry I can't contain it.

"He didn't deserve this," I say.

"There are a lot of things he didn't deserve," Danny responds.

"What does that mean?"

"Nothing. I'm just saying…"

"Saying what?" I ask. "What are you saying?"

He shakes his head. "I don't want to argue with you."

"Oh, you don't? Well, I don't give a fuck what you want. I didn't want to lose my husband. I didn't want to become a widow at thirty-one!" My hands shake.

"Quiet, Bexley."

"Don't you fucking tell me to be quiet!" I shove him and I can't control myself, so I start hitting him on the arms, on the head, everywhere.

"It should have been you!" I scream as tears fall from my eyes. I hit him until my hands ache, until my arms grow tired and he has to stop me.

"It should have been you." I sob as he holds me. "Don't touch me!" I shove away from him. "Stop the car, Johnny."

"Bexley," Danny says, his voice filled with as much pain as I feel.

"I said stop the goddamn car!"

Johnny does as I ask, and I yank open the door, running as fast as I can away from them. The cold wind slaps me in the face and my lungs burn, and then I'm yanked into the air.

"No, no, no," I say, fighting him.

"Please stop, love," he urges me, putting his face in my neck.

My heart freezes like the artic wind has swept over it. I shove him away again, looking at him with rage. My chest heaves, my heart pounds, my soul weeps. "Everything is gone," I say. "Everything."

"Everything is not gone. Life has changed, Bexley. When the apple is ripe, it will fall."

"Don't give me that shit. This didn't have to happen."

"I know," he says. "I'm sorry."

"I loved him, Danny. I loved him."

I cross my arms as the snow falls around us. "I had it all. I had the white fence and everything."

"You'll have it again."

I shake my head. "No. That doesn't happen twice."

"You don't know what the future holds. None of us do."

"This is our future, Bex. I'm going to paint the fence and fix the porch. You want a red door? I'll paint that, too." Samuel holds his arms out, proud of his purchase. I can't help but smile at his excitement. He looks down at me, and in one quick move he scoops me up, twirling me around. I laugh out loud, feeling his scratchy beard against my cheek.

"Put me down." I laugh as my feet hit the ground. He smiles at me, moving my hair away from my cheek. We've been seeing each other for a year now.

"What do you say, Bex? Move in with me?"

I swallow, stopping my mind from thinking about anything but this moment, but it doesn't listen. It's been three years since I've touched Danny, but I still think about him. Even now, as the man who clearly loves me more than anything asks me to share a home with him. He notices the hesitation.

"I can make you happy. Just let me."

"Can we please get back in the car. We need to go," Danny says, bringing me back to the now.

Defeated and knowing I have no other choice right now, I nod, keeping my distance from him.

Once in the car, my thoughts start to wander.

"Why haven't the police contacted me?" I ask as Johnny hits the gas.

"They don't need to."

"Surely they have questions."

"They did, but they don't now."

"Why?"

He sighs. "Because I took care of it."

"You took care of it? What does that mean?"

"It means I paid them off. I don't need them investigating it."

"They can help," I say. He laughs and it infuriates me. "What the fuck is so funny, Danny?"

"What's so funny?" he asks condescendingly, looking over at me.

"Yes."

"What's so funny is the cops are worse than the bad guys. At least the bad guys show you who they are. Cops hide behind their badge, pretending to be angels, but they're wolves in sheep's clothing.

"They confiscate drugs, money, and weapons from the crooks, making the good citizens of America think they're getting it off the streets, but you know what they do, Bexley? They cut the drugs and sell it back to the drug dealers at a higher price.

"They keep the dirty money so they can give their kids a good Christmas and please their wives with jewelry and nice shit. They sell the guns on the black market.

"There's no good guy in this, love. The world is a corrupt place. Everyone is out for themselves. Money talks, and it reveals who people really are. They can't help us, and I don't want them to."

"You're wrong. There was a good guy and he's the one dead."

Danny flinches. It's faint, but I see it. He may know more about the dark side of the world than I do, and maybe that makes me a little naïve, but I know there are still good people out there and now we're one down. I feel so hopeless.

I have so many regrets. I just wish I had the chance to make things right. I wish I had been more honest with Samuel. I wish I loved him like he did me. I wipe my face and look out the window as the snow continues to cover the ground. The sun beams off of it, blinding me.

The sun reflects off the puddle of water outside. I stare out the window of our home. A little drunk, because today was a rough day.

Insurgent

Paul's kid had a birthday party, and I had to be in the same room with Danny. I felt him watching me, lurking in the corner. I felt hot and flustered about it. I don't know why. I found myself wishing for a different life, wishing I was married to him, wishing I was going home with him.

I'd dart my eyes in his direction, and the fierceness there had butterflies soaring in my gut. I needed something. Release, I don't know. I needed him. It's been so long since I felt his rough touch, heard his deep whisper in my ear. Samuel is good, but Danny...Danny is sin and always tasted like a high I could never come down from.

I excused myself from the couch where I sat with Ellen, Paul's wife. Walking past kids in the hallway, I smiled at Samuel as I walked by the kitchen where he and Paul talked. I kept going until I was outside, breathing in fresh air and trying to control this feeling. I'd been around Danny a handful of times over the years, but today...I don't know. It's different. I found myself more drawn to him than I could stand.

I walk around the shed, grabbing a cigarette from my purse. I'm not a big smoker. It's what killed my mom, but sometimes it releases stress. Sometimes it makes me feel closer to her. Closer to

Danny. I don't know. I light the thing, exhaling and holding it away from me so I don't smell.

"I didn't know you smoked," I hear. I look, seeing Danny with his hands in his pockets.

I hit the thing one more time. "I don't."

He grins. "Nice party, huh?"

I shrug. "I guess."

"You okay?" he asks with a tilt of his head.

I don't respond. His eyes go down to my legs. I'm in a sundress, with small heeled sandals.

"You look pretty."

"Thanks," I say, hitting the smoke again. He walks closer to me. I watch, my throat growing dry.

Does he know how much I want him?

Does he know what being around him even after all this time does to me?

I'm still dying.

I still dream about him.

I hate myself.

I hate him.

And then he steps even closer. I can smell his cologne. Feel my heart pound against my neck. Feel his finger as it runs up my thigh.

"Would you stop me if I touched you where he gets to now?" He leans in close to my ear. "Are you happy?" he asks me. I close my eyes, letting out the

shakiest breath. I feel him against my stomach. He wants me as much as I want him.

He makes circles on my skin. "All you have to do is say the word, Bexley. Say you want me."

The wetness in my panties is for him. The beat of my heart is for him. "Will I ever stop?" I say on a whisper. It pains me.

"I hope not," he says.

"Bexley," I hear. It's Ellen. She's probably ready for the cake.

"I need to go."

He steps away from me. I look at him a moment too long. He reaches for the cigarette. I hand it to him, and without another word, I walk away.

Samuel shutting the front door snaps me from thoughts about earlier.

"Hey," he says. "You okay?"

I'd left the party right after the cake cutting, telling him I didn't feel great. He looks down at the drink in my hand before looking back at my face.

"I lied," I say with a guilty smirk. "Kids were giving me a headache."

He gets a crease in his brow, but says, "I get it."

Understanding Samuel.

Still in a sundress, but barefoot, I walk over to the liquor cabinet. "Have a drink with me."

"It's three in the afternoon."

"So?" I ask with a smile.

He shrugs, walking over to me. I pour him a shot. "May your laugh, your love, and your wine be plenty."

"Ditto," I reply. We clink glasses and down the drink.

He smiles. "You a little drunk?"

"Just a little," I say with a grin.

He looks over my face in a loving way.

"Kiss me," I say. And he does and I make it deeper. I grasp his neck and pull him to me, rougher than normal.

He moans into my mouth. "You are a little drunk," he says. I bite my lip.

Moving away from him, I walk over to the dining room table and lift myself onto it. I spread my thighs. He watches. I lift my dress. He swallows. Samuel walks over to me, and then he sinks to his knees. The touch of his tongue against my clit sends a shock to my system. I gasp, grabbing his hair.

He kisses and sucks and fingers me until I come, and then he stands up. Removing his cock, he slowly slides in, but I need it rough. I need...Danny.

I push him away. "Get on the floor," I say.

"Wouldn't the couch be better?"

Insurgent

I shake my head. He does as I ask, and I climb on top of him with my face toward his feet. I reach down and slide him inside of me and he flexes up. I cry out in a moan laced with pleasure. He grips onto my hips and I move with him. My knees dig into the hard floor as I hold on to his thighs.

"Look back at me," he says, but I can't. My eyes are shut. I'm thinking of Danny's finger on my thigh. The smell of his cologne. I rock harder, faster, until sweat is dripping down my back. I feel the rush of my orgasm building, ready to crumble.

"Bexley." He stops. My eyes fly open and I look back. He moves, causing me to get off. "I don't want to do it like this."

"Why?" I ask. "I was about to come."

"We never do it like this."

"So, what's wrong with doing something different?"

"Nothing," he says. "Come on, let's go upstairs. Let me make love to you."

I roll my eyes, frustration warming my chest. "I don't want to make love, Samuel. I want to fuck. I want raw, hard fucking."

He looks at me like I've grown two heads. "What's gotten into you?"

I exhale and shake my head. "Nothing. Let's just forget it." I walk away from him and run up the stairs.

"Bexley," I hear, but I ignore him, shutting the door in our bedroom. I walk over to the dresser, grab my vibrator, and lock the bathroom door behind me. I strip, turn on the shower, and fuck myself, thinking about Danny until I come with his name rushing from my lips.

And then I cry.

"I will fix this. You're safe with me," Danny says, yanking me from years ago.

I wipe at the tears on my face, angry at my thoughts. "I'm no safer with you than I am with the devil," I reply, not looking at him, and we say nothing else.

Chapter Forty-Five

Bexley
2019

"Where are we going?" I ask Danny when we get back to his bar.

"Atlanta," he barks, clearly annoyed at me, like I am at him. He takes a seat on the barstool.

"Where's Trig?" he says to Johnny.

"Said he wasn't feeling well."

He grabs his case of smokes from his front pocket. He lights one, looking over at me when I sit down at one of the tables. His hair is slicked back. He wears a black wool trench coat with a black tailored suit and thin tie. He's handsome. I can't stand him.

I wear a long black coat over a contemporary knee-length black dress, with three-quarter sleeves and a surplice V-neck. My eyes are swollen behind black shades, and my hair is pulled straight back into a ponytail. I skipped makeup, knowing I'd just cry it off. My skin is pale and chapped.

I'm a nightmare, while he's a daydream.

I look at my fingernails, flicking one with the other as Mae walks in from the back.

"Drink anybody?" she asks.

"Whiskey," Danny says. "Bex, you want anything?"

"Wine," I say. "Red, please." And it doesn't go unnoticed that no matter how mad I make this man, he still goes out of his way to make sure I'm happy. A small ping of guilt resolves in my chest, but it doesn't last long.

Mae prepares our drinks and Johnny gets up once they're placed on the bar. "I'm heading home to pack some clothes. Be back shortly," he says.

Danny nods, hitting his cigarillo. Grabbing his drink, he downs it. "Mae, give us some privacy, please."

Mae looks from him to me, and then like a child throwing a tantrum, she tosses down her towel and leaves. I feel guilty. This is her home. She's been here every day with him. I'm an intruder and yet, he tosses her out.

"Aren't you going to grab your drink?" he asks me. I exhale and slide my chair out, walking over to the bar. I choose to sit a stool away from him. I lift my glass.

He smirks slightly at my distance. "We need to go get some things from your house. Clothes and whatever else you need."

"How long will I be gone?"

"I don't know."

"Do you know anything?" I ask.

He looks over at me, not saying anything before he looks away. I taste a sip of my wine, enjoying the sweetness now on my tongue.

Danny reaches over and grabs the liquor bottle, pouring himself another. He picks up his glass. "To Samuel."

I nod, not able to say those words. Silence is welcome and comfortable, but we've never been uneasy around one another. I remove my glasses, rubbing my eyes and sliding a hand over my head.

"This is the way things are going to go," Danny says to me. "You're going to stop with this attitude. You're going to accept the situation we're in, and you're going to be grateful you have me to look out for you."

Fire ignites inside my chest and I feel my cheeks redden. I laugh. "If you believe for one second I'm going to do any of that, then you'll be sadly mistaken." I down my drink and stand up, walking to the stairs, but he reaches and grabs my arm.

"You will do as you're told, Bex," he says.

I narrow my eyes at him. And for a split second, I see the man Danny has grown into. When we were younger and in love, I never for a moment thought he would hurt me. I still don't, but I can see why he seems to be feared and why he demands respect. But it doesn't mean he's getting it from me. I yank from his touch. "I need to stop by the shop first. If we're leaving town, then that's non-negotiable."

"Fine," he says.

And then I turn to face him. "Now, let me tell you how this is going to go. I will follow your lead, simply because I'm clearly in danger. I will try to control my anger toward you and keep my attitude at bay. But I will not be grateful, for there isn't a damn thing to be grateful for at this moment.

"Also, Danny O'Brien, you will not speak to me like I am one of your men. You do not pay me, and you do not, or have you ever, owned me."

I can't imagine what he would do if anyone else spoke to him the way I just did, but what does he do when I do it? He smiles. "Okay, Mrs. O'Brien. Let's change and then we'll go."

Chapter Forty-Six

Trig

"Sweep just left. Meet me at Bones' bar, now. Park on the side," I say into the phone.

"Okay, be there in a few."

Chapter Forty-Seven

Bexley

Later, after we've changed, we pull up to the curb, and both of us step out, walking toward A-Street Flower Shop. Me, now in jeans and a sweater, him, now in jeans and a long-sleeved button-down. Both of us still in black. My mind replays Danny calling me Mrs. O'Brien and, I have to admit, I never thought I'd hear him call me that.

Actually, I did, but only if I was married to him.

It's clear he's always thought of my marriage with Samuel as nothing more than a temporary nuisance. He never gave it the respect it deserved, but I have no doubt if it was us who were married, he would act as if it were law. I roll my eyes at the thought and cross my arms as goosebumps form on my neck when the wind moves my hair, tickling my skin, and then out of nowhere, a man appears and knocks Danny in the head.

"Danny!" I cover my mouth in shock. A masked man hits him a second time. Danny, now on the sidewalk, blinks and then goes to get up, looking completely disoriented.

The man kicks him in the ribs. Not having any idea what to do, I jump on the guy's back, hitting him repeatedly in the head with my fist. Like I'm nothing but a ragdoll, he yanks me off and I hit the ground, and then something hard smacks me in the head.

Everything goes black.

Chapter Forty-Eight

Sweep
(Atlanta)

"You people got a nice place here," Simon says, picking his teeth with a toothpick. He's got an empty plate in front of him, brought in by the staff here at Red from the restaurant next door. The trick to get into the casino below Red is through a broom closet in the kitchen of that said restaurant. They've got good ravioli. The chef talks too much, though, and reminds me of Yaps. I do the signal of the cross in my mind. Poor bastard's food for the worms now.

But that's what happens when you're disrespectful. At least around Bones. My boy's been missing for nearly a month now. I've looked everywhere.

"Yeah, Bones set all this up. Guy who used to own it got busted by the feds. If it weren't for Bones, he'd be in prison."

"Sad thing what happened to Bones. Still no word?" Simon says, leaning back, adjusting his white slacks over his belly.

"No, but we'll find him."

"Hope so. Man's not very friendly, but he's one of those you know you can trust in business."

I don't respond to that. "So, where's the product?"

"Out back. There's a vehicle dressed up like a produce truck near the restaurant. You'll find your cocaine in there."

"Okay," I say. "And there is where I'll leave the money."

He shrugs. "Fine by me." He stands up, dropping the toothpick on the plate. "Are you who I'm doing business with now?"

"For now, yes. But not forever." I stand, too. "I'll be in touch."

"Have some fun," Trig says.

"I think I will," Simon says with a smile. I look over and see Moretti talking with a man I've never seen before.

"Who's he talking to?" I ask Trig.

He shrugs. "Who knows."

I look down at him. "How about you find out, yeah?"

"Fine," he says, getting up. I narrow my eyes at him, then I spot Nugget. Those two never come to Atlanta with us, but this time they decided it was needed. I don't get why. The man Moretti's talking to has dark skin, dark hair, and dark eyes. He wears a set of gold chains around his neck. The old school skinny ones.

Moretti, in a blue tux with a maroon tie, smiles at him. I see Trig walking over to Nugget, who gives him a curious look. The two talk and Nugget looks my way. I lock eyes with him and he smiles. And then he says something else to Trig. Trig looks over at Moretti and the man we don't know, and then he grabs a drink from a bartender as she walks by.

I grow annoyed at his indifference to finding out what the fuck is going on here. He's got just as much time in this business as we do. Moretti could be shoving us out. Simon walks back over to me.

"We've got a problem," he says. "There's an issue with one of our dealers."

"Don't you have men for this?"

"They're tied up. I could use your help. I'll throw in some extra."

I narrow my eyes. "How about you put that extra to the side? Bones and I will grab it the next time we come. And I want the powder that's been stolen."

He grins. "You really think you're going to find him, huh?"

"I know I will. Whoever has him wants something. It's only a matter of time before they come for it."

He nods, lighting a smoke. "So, I got your help then?"

"Yeah. You got my help."

"What's going on here?" Trig asks.

"Looks like those men stole cocaine from a dealer who works for Simon."

"No shit," Trig says. "I mean, why are we here? This isn't our jurisdiction."

"We're doing Simon a favor."

"Oh yeah, and what are we getting out of it?"

"Money. We're getting money that Moretti doesn't know about."

"We're doing something behind his back?"

"Isn't he doing something behind ours? You never did tell me who that man was he was talking to."

"Some guy named Raul."

"What's his deal?" I ask from the car. I can see in the windows of the apartment duplex the men are in. Stupid idiots didn't even close the blinds. Everything they're doing is visible. They're amateurs at best.

They probably spotted Simon's guy selling at one point, so they watched him, and they got the idea they could rob them. Sell all the product at one time to earn some fast cash, not knowing that Simon's men are everywhere, so more than likely they'll be trying to sell back to them.

If we don't get rid of them, Simon's guys will eventually. You want something like this taken care of immediately. It doesn't look good when you have loose ends.

"I don't know," Trig says. "Maybe Moretti has something going on, on the side."

"You don't think that's a problem?" I ask him.

"I think he's allowed to do whatever the fuck he wants."

I lift a brow, toss my smoke out the window, and then say, "Come on."

Getting rid of the guys is no issue. We go in with silencers and shoot the three guys in the back of the head. One tries to run. We get him as he is climbing out the window. It makes it easier on us; we don't have to carry him through the house.

We put them in body bags and find an old cemetery. We dig up a grave from the 1800s, toss them in, throw the dirt back over it, and are on our way. We make it back to Jersey with Moretti and Nugget.

Once back at the clubhouse, Trig takes off to wherever Trig's been taking off to, and I wait for Moretti to head home. I break into his office and go through his desk. I find some information that I don't quite understand and it doesn't sit well.

I find girls' names and then numbers beside them, drivers' licenses, and social security numbers. Odd shit that he has no business having. I pull out my phone and take pictures and then put everything back the way I found it. Once I shut the door, I turn around to see none other than Nugget sitting on the couch.

He just stares at me, leaning over.

I don't move, and he doesn't say anything, and then I snap my fingers. Still nothing.

Walking over to him, I notice his arm is tied and a needle is sticking out. "Jesus Christ, you're doing the fucking heroin?" I take a picture of that, too.

I leave and go home.

Chapter Forty-Nine

Sweep

I stand outside Bones' bar, hitting my smoke as the cold Jersey wind sweeps across my face. I've searched everywhere for Bones. The cops have, too, only because Moretti is paying them otherwise. They don't give a fuck about Danny O'Brien, and it helps that Bexley's uncle has filed a missing person's report.

How can he just disappear? Both him and Bex? Did they plan this? Would he do this and not tell me? He's always had it bad for the girl. He'd mentioned getting out of this lifestyle when Mickey got popped, but I just can't see him not telling me.

We're boys. We're brothers. I've had this guy by my side since we were kids.

A few people walk into the bar. "'Sup, Sweep? Sorry about Bones, man."

I nod, hitting the joint between my fingers as I lean back against the wall, my eyes going to the concrete below me when I hear a truck pull up.

Trig gets out. "Why are you standing out here in the cold, man?" he asks.

"Too many fucking people in there," I say, passing him the joint.

He nods. "You and your introverted ass."

I shrug, looking at his boots. "Have you been playing in the mud?"

He looks down, too, blowing smoke. "Nah, went out to my dad's old hunting cabin."

"What the fuck for?" I ask, looking at his truck and seeing the tires are caked also.

"Needed some space."

"From what?"

"You sure are nosy all of a sudden," he says to me.

"Just never known you to need space."

"What, you're the only one who can be secluded?"

I shrug. "Whatever."

"Anything new come up about our boy?" he asks moments later.

"No. Still nothing."

I want to go into more detail about it with him, but honestly, Trig has been acting weird lately and disappearing for hours at a time. Now he comes here with mud on his tires and boots. I didn't even know his dad had a cabin.

Wait? I didn't even know about his dad.

"You said your dad?" I ask.

He nods, offering me back the joint, but I shake my head. "You've never talked about your family."

"Well, I am now."

"Why were you in the foster home if you had a dad?"

"He's no longer here."

"So, he's dead?"

"That's correct," he says, dropping the joint and putting it out with his boot. "I'm heading in. I need a drink."

I nod, sniffing as he opens the door.

Three days later, I'm heading out of my house. It's early, and the sun has yet to blister the sky with orange and blue light. I stand by the car, breathing in, and then without thinking, I hop into my car and head to Trig's house.

It only takes me moments. He doesn't live far from where I stay. Placing my coffee in the cup holder, I grab a smoke and light it. Rolling the window down a bit, I hit my brakes when I see Trig walking out to his truck with what looks to be coats.

Pulling over, I place my cigarette between my lips and watch as he cranks the truck. His reverse lights come on, and he backs up, hitting the curb before taking off down the street.

And I don't know why—call it a gut feeling, one that has me feeling sick. One that makes me ask myself, *What am I doing? What am I thinking?*

But regardless, I hit the gas and follow him. I'm careful to make sure Trig doesn't see me following him. But I'm always careful. Since day one, my boy and I said, "Never get Caught," and we've yet to do that. Despite the tails we get every once in a while.

We know we're running a big enough operation for the feds to start noticing. The question isn't if they start digging into our business, but when. Bones has Paul keeping an eye on things for us and keeping us informed if he hears anything we should be concerned about.

Bones has been missing for over a month now, and he hasn't seen the shit I've seen. Moretti and Nugget are being shady as fuck. I've run things while Bones has been gone. I've collected money from the businesses in exchange for protection. I've made sure things were running smoothly at the warehouse and that we got our shipment of heroin on time from Miguel, like we're supposed to. I've flown to Atlanta and checked on Red and our cocaine business there.

In this business, there will always be someone trying to one-up you. Trying to take what you have. You must always be ready. That's one reason Bones hardly ever gets intoxicated. He's always told me to *"Be alert. You're always going to have enemies. You must be ready."* I don't know how he's gone. I don't know how he let someone get him.

I won't say he's dead. Not until I see his body. Me following Trig is not right. I trust that man, almost as much as I trust Bones, but he's been shady for a while now, and I don't have a good feeling about it.

I'm usually good at reading people. I'm quiet because I observe. I've noticed the mud on his shoes and tires. I've noticed he disappears sometimes for a while and he never used to do that. He was always at the clubhouse with one of the whores or enjoying the cocaine and too much whiskey. But lately that's not been the case. He's seemed stressed out and unkempt.

I don't trust him any longer. We head out of the city, and I know where we're going. The Pine Barrens. Where we buried Mickey.

I slow, letting a car or two get between us, and then I follow on, making sure not to lose him, but when he begins to cut off from civilization, heading down a dirt road, I have to stop. He could see me. There are no more cars. Nothing to keep me hidden, so I take a breath, light another smoke, and park. I will wait for him to come back.

And then I'll take a drive into the Barrens and check things out for myself.

Chapter Fifty

Trig

I pop my neck, looking ahead at the dirt road that leads to the cabin. It's a run-down shitty thing, but it wasn't always like that. We spent plenty of summers here fishing and hunting. This cabin holds many memories for me. I will kill Bones there and I will toss him in the swamp and let the alligators have him.

Maybe I'll keep Bexley for a while longer. I've tried to get to Paul and their fucking grandmother, but there were too many men protecting them. Bones was right. I couldn't even get close. So, I'm done with this shit. Sweep's ass is getting too nosy, and I know when enough is enough.

So, I won't take everything from him, but I will take his life, and that'll just have to do.

Chapter Fifty-One

Bones
One month three days missing

Thoughts about us and that kiss vanish when we hear the sound of a vehicle coming down the road. There are only windows on the sides, so I can never see the vehicle. I can never see if anyone might be with him or what he may have in his hands. It's a guessing game.

I take a deep breath and calmly exhale as I hold on to the glass from the broken window. I look at Bexley. I hear the crunch of the tires, and then it comes to a stop. The door creaks open and then it shuts, but he leaves the car running like always.

"Are you ready?" I ask her.

She nods, but she looks terrified.

"We got this," I say, trying to reassure her, but I'm not so sure myself. Regardless, I don't let her see my worry. I give her a wink. She smiles, but it's not from happiness. I look at the door. It opens and I plunge the glass straight into his stomach.

Trig grunts, and a gun falls out of his hand. He swings his arm out to hit me, but he misses and falls forward, away from the door.

"Run, Bexley," I say just as he thrusts his body into mine.

I feel the air exit my lungs. Trig moves his fist back and hits me in the face, once, twice. I nearly black out.

A loud gunshot rings through the cabin.

"Get the fuck off him," Bexley says. Trig freezes and I shove him. I stand up and walk over to Bexley.

Trig laughs and shakes his head.

"Why didn't you just shoot him?" I ask her.

"Figured you'd want to handle that."

I feel lightheaded. I sway.

"I told you to run. You never list..."

"Danny?" she says. I look down and see blood. My knees buckle. "Oh God. The glass."

I put my hand there and feel it.

"Watch out!"

Blackness.

To be continued...

Made in the USA
Monee, IL
23 July 2022

10206397R00166